Must Love Black

KELLY McCLYMER

Simon Pulse

New York London Toronto Sydney

This book is a work of fiction. Any references to historical events, real people, or real locales are used fictitiously. Other names, characters, places, and incidents are products of the author's imagination, and any resemblance to actual events or locales or persons, living or dead, is entirely coincidental.

SIMON PULSE
An imprint of Simon & Schuster Children's Publishing Division
1230 Avenue of the Americas, New York, NY 10020
SIMON PULSE and colophon are registered trademarks of Simon & Schuster, Inc.
Designed by Cara E. Petrus
The text of this book was set in Aldine.
Manufactured in the United States of America
First Simon Pulse edition September 2008
10 9 8 7 6 5 4 3 2
Library of Congress Control Number 2008921517
ISBN-13: 978-1-4169-4903-9
ISBN-10: 1-4169-4903-8

Must Love Black

ALSO BY KELLY McCLYMER

To Brendan—
my not-goth boy in black

ACKNOWLEDGMENTS
My thanks to Nadia, Anica, Michelle, Annie, and Mike,
who all helped me reach my inner goth.

CHAPTER ONE

Your intractable independence is a state of heart and mind, I fear, Addie. Not something to be cured, but something to be endured.
—Lady Margaret to Miss Adelaide Putnam,
Manor of Dark Dreams, p. 3

I learned a long time ago that the most insignificant-seeming thing may cause big change. The butterfly effect, it's called, according to Mr. Heck, who taught ninth-grade social studies like he knew every butterfly that ever broke out of a chrysalis, but only liked the really pretty ones (i.e., the brightly colored ones).

Me? I asked if there's any such thing as an all-black butterfly. He said, "Butterflies don't do goth." Naturally, the rest of the class laughed. I wanted to prove him wrong. But when I searched the Internet, I only found a few "black" butterflies with lots of yellow, green, and white. Oh, and a rock band and a movie. I guess I wasn't the only one who wished there were some solid-black butterflies in the world.

Whenever anyone asks me why I like to wear black, or calls me "goth girl" (I'm not), or asks if I'm auditioning to be a stagehand or a mime (yeah, right), or tells me to get pierced (no extra holes needed, thankyouverymuch), I just shrug and say, "I like to be prepared. Black covers everything from prom night to the end of the world." Most people are wise enough to blink twice and move on.

"Be prepared for the butterfly crap of life to drop on you at any moment" is my motto, which was why I was able to watch without drama, as my dad and stepmother (thirty minutes and counting) danced their first dance as a married couple. Almost.

I condensed my feelings into a single snarky comment to my best friend, Sarah. "If this was a horror movie, now comes the moment when she kills him and inherits it all. Whatever *all* is."

Sarah, looking as comfortable in her frilly emerald and pomegranate dress as I felt uncomfortable in my shiny pink bridesmaid gown, happily took up the game. "If it was a romantic movie, this would be the moment when they walk off into the sunset and she makes him as happy as your mom did."

"Not a chance. Mom and Dad were perfect for each other." I watched Krystal (who names their kid Krystal?) laugh and blush as my dad dipped her and kissed her nose. "If this was a science fiction movie, she'd be an alien or a mannequin."

"As stepmothers go, she seems pretty much human." Sarah was highly influenced by her do-gooder parents to think positive thoughts. It was a wonder we'd become friends.

"Wait until they come back from their honeymoon cruise

extravaganza. I'll never be able to eat another apple without wondering if she's poisoned it."

"Poisoning apples is so last millennium," Sarah teased. "If you're that worried about the insurance money, you should have gone on the cruise with them instead of taking that weirdo nanny-to-the-spoiled-rich-kids summer job."

"Right. I already feel like the third wheel from nine to five, do I need to make it twenty-four/seven?"

"Don't let it bother you," Sarah said.

"I'm not." I turned away from the sight of the happy couple; the image of my dad's bright smile lingered a little against my eyelids as I blinked. "It's his life."

"You only have to deal until you finish high school." Sarah always liked to point out the silver lining to the garbage heap of life.

"Hey, I'm free of the lovebirds for the summer. Maybe by the time they come back, they'll be done with the kissing and cuddling, and life can get back to normal."

"Maybe you'll like her living in the house?"

"Doesn't matter whether I like it or not, she'll be there, just like a cockroach, a spider, and a fly—all rolled up together."

Sarah waved her hand and laughed. "Even if she pulls two ugly daughters out of the closet after she gets back from the honeymoon, at least you know you have only one year left before you head to college."

It stung that my best friend on the planet didn't understand how terrible my life had become. "Thanks for the cheer-up. You almost match my dress for nauseatingly bright and—"

Again with the hand flap. "You look pretty in pink."

"Don't ever say that again." I had known this day was going to be bad, but I'd thought Sarah would be in my corner. Instead, she kept piling on the sun and light.

"When I get married, my matron of honor will wear black." I grinned as I said it, knowing that the very thought would make her hyperventilate.

She grinned back, her gotcha grin. "Don't you mean *maid* of honor? And I thought you weren't getting married."

"I never said I wasn't getting married. Just that it isn't my raison d'être like it is for some people." I nodded toward the happy couple on the dance floor. "And I meant matron of honor. You'll be married way before I am. You're not nearly as discriminating."

"True." Sarah didn't even blink at the dis. She takes the seesaw approach to what people think. If it matters to her, she cares; if not, she doesn't. That's why I put up with a girl who likes pink and thinks happy rainbow thoughts 99.9 percent of the time. "But I hope by that time you'll have stopped hating all the colors of the rainbow."

Sigh. Rainbow thoughts again. "Spare me. Rainbows are for people who don't know the dark side of life."

"On the contrary, rainbows are for people who do know the dark side of life. Rainbows come after the storm, remember? At some point you have to live your life and let go of your grief."

Easy for her to say. "Thanks. I thought you were supposed to be the sensitive one. Word of advice: Don't tell the folks you're building the house for this summer that you think they ought to get over being poor and dance around the empty lot."

She frowned. One thing Sarah cares about is doing positive things in the world. "They'll be working hard to build their home along with us, you know. It's part of the deal. You should come. Ditch the nanny gig and learn some useful skills. Do a little good for real people instead of spoiled brats."

Trust Sarah to point out the potential flaw in my summer plans. "You really think they'll be spoiled brats?"

"Count on it." She ticked off on her fingers: "One, nanny; two, mansion on the coast of Maine; three, nanny."

I shrugged. "It's only for the summer. And who knows, maybe Krystal will come back with her wicked stepmother badge shining and that little summer job nest egg will keep me from having to smile and play nice with mice and birds."

"Hey! Show the 'Rella some respect."

"Never. Girls who voluntarily wear pink and blue should have to dance on top of birthday cakes forever."

"You really are cranky, aren't you?" Sarah gave up trying to cheer me up as suddenly as she'd given up eating meat in the eighth grade, and with the same solemn frown. "I'm sorry for you. But your dad does look happy. I hope someday we'll both find guys who make us feel that special."

I rolled my eyes. "Says the girl who has a new crush every Tuesday."

"You have to kiss a lot of frogs." As usual, she was unashamed of her fickle heart.

"I don't need a guy. Guys make everything complicated. I like simple."

"Sure you do. Two spoiled brats and a posh spa business

run by a rich family that will treat you like a slave. Sounds like a perfectly simple summer to me."

"Money," I countered.

"Mercenary." In Sarah's eyes there was nothing worse than doing something for money. She did, however, make an exception for raising money for a worthy cause.

"Practical." I hadn't been raised by starry-eyed do-gooder parents. I knew I'd have to support myself in this world. Couldn't count on anyone else in life. Money trumped pretty fairy tales any day of the week.

My aunt Faith interrupted our debate, holding a glass of champagne. She had her pity-poor-Philippa look in her eye. "Your mother would be glad he's found a good woman, honey." Aunt Faith always knew what to say to make me want to go hide in a closet. She ruffled my hair. "You know she wouldn't wish him to be lonely forever, right?"

There was only one way to deal with Aunt Faith when she'd had too much champagne and got soppy: run. I stood up and hugged her quickly. "You're right. Thanks. I have to go to the ladies' room."

I didn't even turn to see if Sarah was following me as I made my escape from the tables of laughing guests that circled the dance floor. I knew that she would.

"You can't hide in the bathroom forever," she said as we reached the foyer.

Fortunately, I didn't have to find out whether Sarah was right. Just at that moment, a guy wearing a chauffeur's uniform walked into the reception hall. "Hey, my ride is here."

"Cute." Sarah's standard reaction to any guy under

twenty-five. "I thought he was going to pick you up at your dad's house later."

"That's what Dad wanted. I changed the plans." I looked down at the pink scallops of my skirt and panicked a little. "I don't want him to see me like this."

"Why not? You look nice." Sarah couldn't take her eyes off the guy. "And he looks hot, even in the monkey suit."

"Go tell him so while I turn myself back into a pumpkin. And tell him I'll be right out." I headed for the bathroom to change out of my wedding gear and back into my normal clothes.

Sarah barged in while I was balling up the pink monstrosity and stuffing it into the dinky little garbage can. Her eyes were a little starry from the onset of crush number 10,003 as she said, "Wow. Maybe you have a better deal going on than I thought. Can you ask if they need another nanny?"

"What happened to doing good in the world?"

"I could do some good with him." She wiggled her eyebrows at me suggestively.

Her man-killer act might have worked if I didn't know that she'd only been out on five real dates. Ever. And two of those were pity dates that she'd agreed to because she believed in rooting for the underdog, even if he had acne and the social skills of a seagull. "One day you're going to have to stop talking and start doing, you know," I said.

"Careful, he's not even yours and you're acting all possessive."

I threw a few paper towels on top of the dress to hide it—nothing would be worse than someone seeing it and rescuing it. I'm sure Krystal and my dad would be annoyed that I'd thrown it away. I was gambling that by the time they came home from the honeymoon, the dress would be a distant memory and I could get away with a vague excuse like "I haven't seen it all summer." I had to risk it—no way I was going to keep a reminder of this day hanging in my closet. "He isn't mine. He isn't going to be. You know he has a girlfriend. Guys like that are always taken—even if they're complete jerks." Back in black, I felt like myself. Just because the guy was a hottie didn't mean I had to melt.

"He didn't seem like a jerk," Sarah argued.

"Of course not. He's just doing his job."

"I'm just relieved that he seems seminormal. That 'must love black' thing in the nanny ad creeps me out. It's like you're working for the Addams Family or something. Anyone who loves black as much as you—or who'd make it a job requirement—is weird. Even you can't argue with that."

"I like weird. Why do you think you're my best friend?" Fortunately, we'd left the privacy of the bathroom and were approaching the hottie, so she was too preoccupied with staring at him to answer me.

I was surprised by how much I agreed with Sarah. This guy didn't even look dorky in his uniform. The hat was a bit much, but it made his serious expression seem sexy rather than stuck-up. I smiled at him. "Hi. I'm Philippa."

He nodded. "Geoff."

Man of few words, was he? Good. I picked up my duffel bag from the corner where I'd stashed it when Dad wasn't looking, pointed to my suitcase, and said, "I'm ready if you are."

He looked surprised, and so did Sarah. They both said, at the same time, "Don't you want to say good-bye to your dad?"

I didn't even look behind me. "He's busy."

Sarah protested. "It looks like they're about to cut the cake."

"My cue to cut out, then." I looked at Sarah, trying to will her to understand why I didn't want all the hugs and fatherly admonishments that would no doubt accompany saying good-bye to my dad. "Tell him bye for me, okay?"

Sarah followed me out, looking for a second like she would argue, but then she stopped and stared. Geoff was holding open the back door of a sleek black limo. Her mouth dropped open. "Double whoa! Did you think you were picking up a celebrity?" She flirted a little with Geoff, who smiled back a tiny bit. I think. Impressive. Most guys can't resist the patented Sarah Flirty Smile. The good girl with a hint of mischief.

I smirked and made sure not to look the least bit impressed by the ride. "Still think my summer is going to be worse than yours?"

"You haven't met the kids yet," she reminded me with a grin as she came in for a hug. She was a real hugger, and I tolerated it because I wasn't going to see her for the summer. She took the opportunity to whisper in my ear, "I expect a full update every chance you get." And then she pinched my shoulder. "Go give your dad a hug."

I climbed into the limo instead and was met by the pleasant smell of leather and something spalike: lavender or jasmine or sage or something. I waved as Geoff closed the door. We both ignored Sarah's slight frown. I don't think she'd believed

I would go without saying good-bye. She was wrong. I kind of hoped Dad would run out and catch me before we pulled away. But he didn't.

In the limo I stretched out, trying to pretend I was used to such luxury. I didn't want Geoff to think I was a dork, but I couldn't help doing a double take on reality. I pulled out my job-offer letter, just to make sure I wasn't stuck in a half nightmare, half dream. Never hurts to double-check—and Sarah wasn't around to make fun of me.

"Miss Philippa Munson." Fancy crisp paper, my address in neat calligraphy. I remembered when it came, back when I wasn't sure how I was going to escape the fate of being third wheel on an around-the-world honeymoon, how I'd run my finger around the stiff edge of the envelope, wanting to know what the letter said before I actually ripped open the envelope and read it. My stomach had been in knots and I'd hoped really hard that things would work out. I felt the same way now as the limo hummed along the roads and I stared out the tinted windows as I left the familiar behind. What would my summer be like? The ad I'd answered to get the nanny gig hadn't given much away: NANNY FOR 10-YR-OLD TWINS. MAINE COAST. OWN ROOM & GENEROUS SALARY. SEND HANDWRITTEN LETTER & REFERENCES TO CHRYSALIS CLIFF, BOX 781. MUST LOVE BLACK.

My cell rang and I fished it out of my pocket. Dad. I thought about not answering, but even I couldn't be that cold. "What's up?"

"Sarah said you've left with the chauffeur from Chrysalis Cliff." He sounded tired, like I'd managed to steal the happiness from his day. I tried not to be glad about that.

"I didn't want to bother you. You and Krystal were busy doing the married couple thing, you know?"

"I would have liked to say good-bye to you. To meet this young man—"

I cut him off, knowing he could lecture like this for a long time. "You already talked to everyone at Chrysalis Cliff, plus the Johnsons and the Benfords as references. You know I'll be fine."

"It isn't every day that my daughter starts her first job." He sounded so unhappy that I felt guilty for being glad he cared. "I would have liked to hug you one more time before I go on my honeymoon."

"We'll hug when you get back. You have fun, I'll work hard, and we'll have lots to tell each other at the end of the summer, right?" He'd like that, the idea that I'd actually tell him things about my life.

He sighed. "I love you, honey. If this doesn't turn out well, you have the ship's emergency number to reach me, right?"

"Sure thing." I patted my duffel, as if he could see me. "Have fun on the honeymoon. Don't do anything I wouldn't do."

"Philippa—"

I ended the call and switched off the phone. If he remembered to ask about our call being cut off next time we talked, I'd just say I lost the signal. What could he say to that? It happened a lot around here.

I looked around. The limo was great, but there wasn't a TV or a fridge or anything. Impatience clawed at me as I tried to picture Chrysalis Cliff. Sarah's always on my case about my major personality flaw . . . well, second to the "flaw" of preferring black. I always want to be where I'm going without actually having to "get" there. When we drove to Disneyland on my sixth birthday—a twenty-eight hour drive—I wanted to be there after the first ten minutes in the car. My memory of that trip is a surreal blend of Mom endlessly promising that McDonald's was only a few miles away, and a marathon search for South of the Border signs as we slogged from Maine through North Carolina, the longest state ever. And the teacups. I loved the teacups, whirling, spinning, my head snapping and my hair flying.

Mom used to try to help me with the "problem" of my impatience with this sage advice: "Use your waiting time to enjoy the people show." She was a pretty patient person. She was a history teacher who wanted to be a writer, and I'd watched as she wrote a few pages a day for a year, stacking the paper up, making me wash my hands free of lollipop or peanut butter residue before I could pat and flip and sniff the freshly printed pages in fascination as the stack grew fatter in very slow motion.

After she died I got good at watching the people show. In the first days after the accident it was all I did, sit in my living room and watch the strangers who called themselves friends and family cry, laugh, cart dishes in and out. Most of them glanced at me, frowned, and then left me in my corner with my book. Some brought me food—chicken fingers from KFC or homemade macaroni and cheese. I learned there are as many ways to make macaroni and cheese as there are people in the world. I like the baked kind, with sharp cheese and fat soft noodles.

I found that the great thing about people-watching is if

you just look at people when they talk to you, absorbing the scent of their nervous sweat, watching the way their lipstick gets bitten off in interesting patterns, they eventually stop talking and move away.

Dad didn't push me to put on a happy face or talk about my feelings or cry it all out. I think he understood. When the whirling teacups come to a stop, you have to stay where you are while the world rights itself. Disney staff didn't let us do that on the teacup ride—there were other kids waiting—but life isn't as well organized as Disney, so my dad and I, we stayed still a long time after the crash.

Maybe that was why it hurt that he'd gotten back to "normal"—whatever normal is—with Krystal. How could he forget Mom like that? I never would.

After a quick look to make sure I was out of the line of sight of Geoff's rearview mirror, I took out the battered copy of Mom's book, *Manor of Dark Dreams*, and looked into the green eyes of the woman on the cover. They stood out against the shades of gray of the fog that reached for her, the stone manor house brooding in the distance. It was almost as if Mom were with me. Except that Mom would have been laughing at me for being so impatient when I was living the high life in the back of a limo for the first time ever.

There was only one problem: You can't see a lot from the back of a limo. I leaned forward and tapped on the glass between Geoff and me.

"Yes?" His voice came from a speaker by my ear and I almost squealed.

"Stop the car. I want to sit up front."

There was a second of silence during which I wondered if he would do as I asked. I didn't like the idea of being forced to sit back here without being asked. So I was relieved when he said, "Okay," and pulled over so I could get into the front seat beside him. Much better. Sarah would have given me a thumbs-up for sure.

CHAPTER TWO

Leaning back in the front seat, my duffel on my lap, I slowly got used to the dizzy feeling of launching into the great unknown, in silence. Apparently Geoff wasn't a big talker or in a big hurry. Or maybe he was distracted by the fog we hit somewhere on Route 3, though his hands rested on the wheel with loose confidence. Maybe Sarah could have gotten him talking, if she'd been here. But I wouldn't have bet on it. He seemed very happy to drive like he was the only one in the limo. It should have made me feel invisible, but instead I felt an electric buzz between us that made my skin tingle. Great. Just what I needed to complicate the summer—a hot crush vibe.

The big limo purred through the night as if it knew the

route so well it didn't require a driver to maneuver in the heavy fog. Inside, I wasn't purring with the same confidence. Besides the fact that I was a little spooked out by the vibe, I wanted to be there already—like I said, I'm flawed that way.

Mom's advice about people-watching wasn't helpful right now. Except for Geoff, who was driving, and the fog, there wasn't anyone or anything to watch. That left only the dangerous territory of my mind. I could wander the shadow valleys of the past, trying to imagine what my mom would have said about Dad and Krystal's wedding. Or I could peek into the dark corners of the future: living in a strange house, stuck there for the summer, in charge of ten-year-old twins and dreaming of kissing Geoff. Problem was, I really didn't want to go to either place. I knew exactly what I wanted: to be about a day in the future. A nanny already, without the inevitable awkward introductions and stumbling-around-figuring-things-out stage. Too bad I didn't have a time machine handy.

It occurred to me that not only could a time machine get me past the whole introduction part of the summer, I could dial it to get me past the job and back home. I enjoyed imagining how nice it would be to get paid for the job without remembering a thing about it, the one teeny problem being that I still didn't have a time machine at my disposal. Not to mention that sending myself home to the future would mean jumping right into life with Krystal. Not a plus.

I sighed and Geoff looked over at me for a second. He didn't say anything and he'd only looked quickly, but his look made me realize I needed to buck up. Sure, I was going where no one knew me and I had to impress, but I could handle two kids for the summer.

I reached into my bag and thumbed the dog-eared pages of Mom's book, knowing I'd get through the waiting stage, just like I always had—or I wouldn't. Not really my call, which is one big reason why waiting stinks.

I knew what had made me take the chance on this job, a job offered to me on the strength of my babysitting references and a single letter of application—a handwritten letter, at that, in this day and age of DSL and instant messaging. I hadn't questioned it until now, as the silence started pressing against my eardrums. Before, the job had seemed perfect.

It was the last line of the ad that had tipped me over to digging out a sheet of the nice stationery I'd gotten for my birthday from Sarah. "Must love black." It's like the ad had been written just for me, by someone who got that black is practical, black is dependable, and black is *real*. I had known instinctively that Krystal—I refuse to call her Mom—would freak if I worked at a place like that. After I'd been offered the job, she'd actually tried to convince me to work in Bar Harbor instead.

I'd said, no, thank you. Bar Harbor's a happening place for jobs—if you want to be a waitress, a store clerk, or a babysitter of grown tourists on a whale-watching tour. I knew I didn't. I'd been there plenty, when my dad and I had gone to the coast to hike the trails in Acadia National Park and stand on the rocky face of Cadillac Mountain. Lots of high school and college kids spend summers there, stocking, selling, and waiting on customers, being all smiley helpful. I'm better known for my well-timed scowl.

"Must love black," to me, was a promise that I wouldn't have to say "Have a nice day!" sixty times in a row or spend the summer pretending life is all about rainbows. But now that I was on my way to the nanny job, I realized I didn't know the first thing about it.

I looked over at Geoff, wondering if I'd lose points with him by asking questions. Sarah would be thumbs-up for the idea. But Sarah wasn't here.

I pulled my duffel bag a little closer—I'd left it on my lap in the hope that if the limo somehow slid off the road and down a rocky cliff in the fog, I'd be a little protected. The roads around here are a tad narrow and a lot winding, and I'm superstitious that way, what can I say? My voice sounded too loud in the quiet of the car. "So, what are the kids like?"

Geoff shrugged, which made me realize how broad his shoulders were under that dorky uniform. Maybe I'd been a little hasty to dismiss the whole idea of complicating the summer with a guy. "I'm primarily the gardener. The limo driver deal is just for when the full-time guy is off. Like today."

"That doesn't really answer my question about the kids."

"They don't go outside much, and we don't talk when I drive them places."

Okay, I wasn't that fond of the outside, either, so that suited me, except for the part about not seeing Geoff much. He didn't say a lot, but he was good eye candy, even in dork dress. Sarah would no doubt give him a ten on the hotness scale. I hoped he couldn't tell that I was checking him out. "Are they TV addicts? My best friend's little sister watches those Nickelodeon and Disney shows all day long."

He turned on the windshield wipers to get rid of condensation from the fog. "There aren't any TVs at Chrysalis Cliff."

"What? No TV?" That hadn't been in the ad. Of course, the handwritten-letter thing could have been a clue that my employer was not part of the twenty-first century. Maybe I should have asked a few more questions. "That sucks."

Geoff grinned at me. "All the nannies think so, but you're the first to say so." Yep. Definitely a ten. Maybe even an eleven. Good thing Sarah was occupied hammering and sawing for the summer—four states away.

"So, did you have to apply for the job the old-fashioned way too?"

He looked surprised. "Old-fashioned?"

"You know. Handwritten letter. On paper. Instead of over the Internet."

"Oh." He shrugged. "My dad knew somebody who knew somebody who knew that Mr. P needed a gardener. No paper, just an in-person interview." He grinned. "I guess you could say I got my job the really old-fashioned way—through nepotism."

I laughed. "Did they ask if you like black?"

He squinted at me. "I'm a gardener. Why would they ask that?"

"Good point." I would have been happier about seeing Geoff unfreeze slightly, if it weren't for the "all the nannies" phrase. Oh, and if we weren't in an impenetrable fog, going about ten miles under the speed limit on one of those scary winding and steep coastal Maine roads. "No offense, but shouldn't you have your eyes on the road?"

He stopped smiling and turned back to the road, or more like the fog, and we were once again sitting in silence punctuated by the intermittent thunk of the windshield wipers. Geoff's hands had tensed on the wheel. Whoops. He didn't like my questioning his driving skills. No shock there, what guy does?

Krystal says if I learned to express myself more politely—and to smile more—I'd have an easier time in life. Maybe she's right. Because it doesn't occur to me that guys don't like to be criticized until after I've insulted what may be the only cute guy even close to my age at my new job.

My turn to shrug. "Sorry. I'm hyper. I was in a car accident when I was nine."

He didn't answer. So I reached out to turn on the radio and get rid of the silence that was making me think way too much about things I couldn't change. Only . . . "There's no radio?"

He hung a sharp right, guided by a sign that loomed up out of the fog and disappeared too quickly for me to read. "Mr. Pertweath believes TV and radio create noise that keeps us from hearing our inner voices."

"O-kay." This was going to be different. After my mom died, my dad and I never turned off the TV, even when we left the house. And the car radio was permanently tuned to public broadcasting. "Good thing to know. I guess I'll make sure to hide my iPod during the welcome-to-the-job pat down."

He didn't look at me, but his grip on the wheel loosened. "Books. The twins like books."

"Books? I like to read too." That didn't sound so bad. So many kids I babysat for had hated reading. I'd had to play board games with them—or worse, video games. The ones where you can shoot things aren't so bad, except that I always die five minutes into the game. But if these were the kind of kids who can sit still and read to themselves for hours, my summer might not be so bad—especially if I could convince them to read outside, in the garden, so their nanny could flirt with the hottie gardener.

Geoff turned the wheel sharply to the right again and pulled through a gate, so close to the stone column on my side that the shrouded granite passed inches from my nose on the other side of the car window, not even softened by the fog.

The teacups started whirling again as I realized we were here. My job. The fog made reality seem like a dream. I couldn't see the house where I was going to work, only the slight glow of the lights. A pair of fancy double doors, illuminated by lanterns on either side, glowed more and more brightly through the fog until the limo stopped with a crunch of gravel and a lurch.

I couldn't see well through the fog, but the word "loom" loomed in my mind, and I felt as if the pressure of the fog added to the pressure of the silence until my head felt filled with cotton. I opened the door of the limo and jumped out before Geoff had a chance to get out and around to hold open my door.

I stood there, holding my stuffed black duffel bag and

looking at the doors. Walking through them would end the wait I'd endured on the drive here. Time for the teacups to start whirling all over again. Would I like the twins? Would they like me? The chill of the fog touched my face and I couldn't move. The doors were so big that Geoff easily could have driven the limo through them if they were open.

I didn't turn around to look at him. I was too afraid I'd see him grinning at my hesitation. "Maybe I should go around to the servants' entrance?"

"Havens said to drop you off at the front tonight. So here you go." He pulled open the double doors, and then, maybe as payback for my "eyes on the road" comment, he said, "Don't worry, you'll get used to the place . . . if you don't run away crying in the middle of the night like the last nanny."

"Thanks." I paused one second as I smiled at him, and then added, "For keeping your eyes on the road—most of the time."

He didn't take offense—I don't think—because he said, in a stage whisper, "If you need a TV fix, just pay me a visit over the garage."

I proceeded through the door, wondering if a ten had just hit on me—or suggested I was too weak to live without TV. Too bad Sarah wasn't here to interpret guyspeak for me.

And then I had a Dorothy moment and wondered if I'd stepped into Oz. A tasteful, serene Oz, minus Munchkins—and wicked witches, I hoped. The fog had been left behind at the front door. The entry hall was all gleaming cream and peach and tan marble, with a huge chandelier that lit every corner. It was like something from a Jane Austen novel. Except for the gothish girl standing front and center.

A man in a suit came toward us. "Welcome to Chrysalis Cliff, Miss. I'm so glad Geoff brought you safely. The fog is terrible tonight." I thought he was the dad for one second, but the "Miss" clued me in before I said something stupid. This had to be the Havens that Geoff had mentioned, probably the butler or something.

"Geoff drove like there was no fog at all," I said truthfully.

Havens nodded smoothly, with just the faintest hint of a wince. "He's very familiar with the roads." For a stuffy butler type, Havens didn't seem too taken aback by my appearance. But then again, in a place like this he was probably trained not to show a reaction to anything odd. For some reason the tranquil setting and calm butler (not to mention the hot gardener still standing there with my suitcase) made me feel more out of place rather than less. When I feel out of place I tend to make awkward remarks, such as, "So. Do you need to see ID? Or is this proof enough I'm the new nanny?" I gestured to my jeans, top, and duffel bag—all black.

"No ID required." Havens smiled, but it was one of the inscrutable kinds of smiles. I hate those because I don't know what to do—attack, retreat, or just smile in return and feel welcomed. I was tired after a day of watching my dad get married, so I opted to smile back as inscrutably as I could manage.

"Great. Where do I stow my stuff?" Havens's face betrayed nothing of his personality. Was he a closet snob? Did he judge on appearance alone? Would he judge me? "Goth" doesn't cut it when it comes to a word that describes me. I'm complex. Complicated. No one gets me, and I like it that way. Because nothing's permanent. One second your mom's squeezing your hand and you're squeezing hers back. And the next second she isn't squeezing anymore. Then it's only you squeezing and her letting go. Sucks. You can tell yourself the doctors will bring her back, but they won't. They try, but they can't.

Havens reached for my duffel bag, but I stepped out of range. "I've got it." I looked back at Geoff to see if he was laughing at me. But he was watching me with a curious expression. Probably calculating how long I would end up staying.

Not wanting to be like all the other nannies, I decided then and there to stay put, no matter what. It wasn't for Geoff. It wasn't for the money. And it wouldn't matter if the twins turned out to be the brattiest kids on the entire coast of Maine. I would stay because I am *me*: headstrong, coffee loving, black clad, and as stubborn as I wanna be. I raised my chin and shifted my duffel. "Ready when you are."

Havens was such a good butler, he didn't fight me for the duffel bag, or even make a comment about my death grip on the strap. He just held out his hand to indicate where I should walk and said, "Geoff, please carry the rest of the bags in. Miss, this way to your domain."

CHAPTER THREE

I realized I had entered a world in which I would be treated as if I deserved more than my humble birth dictated, at least for the duration of my employment. The realization was not entirely comfortable.

—Miss Adelaide Putnam, *Manor of Dark Dreams*, p. 8

My domain? Whoa. I followed Havens up the wide, curved marble staircase and down a darkened, hushed hallway. I thought about pinching myself to make sure I wasn't dreaming. Running lights glowed softly along the edges of the plush carpet that swallowed my feet and muffled the sounds I made as I walked—Havens was as silent as a ghost.

We stopped at the end of the hall, and Havens swiped a magnetic card to open an elegant old-fashioned cage elevator. The card swipe and the beep that followed it were the only things that kept me from feeling like I'd gone back to the turn of the twentieth century. The question, I guess, was whether I'd walked into Jane Austen's or Jane Eyre's world.

Havens pushed the gold button marked "3." "I'm so sorry that Mr. Pertweath could not greet you himself this evening. But perhaps that was for the best. We welcomed a new set of guests today, and Mr. Pertweath has been very busy. He will have more time to speak with you tomorrow. This will give you a chance to get settled in and get a good night's rest before you begin your duties."

"So the children are in bed?" You never know. I'd babysat for kids with a 7 p.m. bedtime and kids who were allowed to stay up to wait for their parents to get home at 1 a.m.

"Their bedtime is scheduled for eight-thirty," he said. "It is now half past nine. I'm sure they have already retired." The elevator stopped moving and there was a pause for the well-oiled door to be pulled open.

"What time should I wake them in the morning?" I had to wonder if this proper butler thought the kids' bedtime was too early, too late, or just right. When I was ten I didn't have a bedtime. Of course, a set bedtime would have been useless because I had a terrible case of insomnia—sleep isn't very restful when you keep reliving a car accident.

"The children are scheduled to wake at seven. I expect you're tired, but in case you missed dinner in your haste to meet Geoff, I requested that Cook send up a small evening meal for you. You'll find it in the dumbwaiter. That's also where breakfast and lunch for you and the girls will arrive. Dinner will be served in the main dining room."

"Thanks. My dad got married today and I didn't get much of a chance to eat at the wedding. It was so crazy." Crazy being mostly that Krystal had picked out fancy inedible food like anchovy paste miniquiches and scallops wrapped in bacon.

The elevator door opened onto a big room with a wooden floor that creaked reassuringly when we stepped out of the elevator. Havens held the elevator open with one hand and waved toward a door on the right. "Your room is through there, and the twins are there." He waved to the left.

Havens pointed to a round table where a thin black binder was centered. "I've provided you with an elevator key card and a copy of the daily schedule, as well as some reading material about the spa here at Chrysalis Cliff, so you'll be prepared when you meet with Mr. Pertweath tomorrow morning to discuss your duties as pertaining to Triste and Rienne."

"Great." Yeah, great. My four years of French and an English-speaking waiter could get me a cup of coffee in Paris. Still, I was pretty sure the twins' names meant "sad" and "nothing." No wonder the ad had specified "must love black." It had seemed like an omen. I wondered if I'd been a little too hasty deciding it was a good omen.

Havens glanced at the closed door of the twins' bedroom as if wondering if it would open. Ah. So maybe they weren't the perfectly scheduled robots his description had suggested. Was that good or bad? I waited for the door to open so I could tell. It stayed shut. Havens turned back to me and said, "I'm afraid the children are asleep, so you'll have to wait until morning to meet them."

"That's fine." More than fine considering what Geoff had said about previous nanny runaways.

Havens nodded as if he might possibly believe I was perfectly competent to handle whatever came next. The elevator doors opened smoothly and Havens stepped on just as Geoff came out carrying my one little suitcase. When they closed behind him, Havens was gone.

Wow. Alone with a hottie in my own domain. And just this morning I was wondering if life would ever improve from pink taffeta and a newly married father. Who could have guessed?

Geoff carried the suitcase into my bedroom, set it down, and emerged again without saying a word. I was so wound up from the wedding, the quiet ride with Geoff, and the need not to look like a dork in front of the butler that I couldn't relax. I had to fight the urge to wander and touch everything I saw.

Geoff pushed the elevator button and waited quietly. I had to find a way to make this guy talk.

"So, do you like working for Mr. Pertweath?"

He shrugged. "It's a good job—and he gives me time off to take classes at U Maine during the school year."

A college boy. Sarah would be drooling. "What's your major?"

"Horticulture, with a minor in Wildlife Ecology."

"Cool. So you want to be a gardener for real, after you graduate?"

Again with the shrug. "I'd like to be a game warden maybe. But I get a lot of chances to work outdoors here"—he tugged at his uniform collar—"except when I'm a back-up driver."

The elevator dinged before I could ask anything else. "See you around," I said. I enjoyed the display of bicep flex when he pulled open the inner cage door and stepped into the elevator.

"See you," he echoed as the door slid closed. I hoped that was a promise.

I looked around, suddenly feeling the silence like a blanket over me. This place was posh. A domain. Even Addie, the nanny in my mother's book, hadn't dreamed of a domain. Just a schoolroom with a few books and a cat that dozed by the fire. Looking around, I saw lots of high-tech computer equipment, expensive furniture, and shelves full of books. No TV, just as Geoff had said. I'd have to catch up on my favorite shows on the Internet. Or maybe I would psych myself up to take Geoff up on his offer of watching TV at his place.

I didn't see any signs of a pet. No gerbil cage, no cat or dog bed, no fish tank. That was good. Pets were more trouble than they were worth. And then they died.

I checked out the books' spines. Classics, of course. Dickens. Austen. The Brontës. Hemingway and Fitzgerald. Shakespeare in a leather-bound set. Aesop's fables in an illustrated version that I couldn't help thumbing through. *Bulfinch's Mythology*, again illustrated, but with the tiniest text I'd ever seen. Weren't Triste and Rienne only ten? Maybe these books were for when they were older? No encyclopedia, but given the computers, that wasn't too surprising. *Harry Potter* was the only modern spot in a classic world. Lots of stuff on ghosts and spirituality—which probably explained the three game tables: one with a Ouija board; one with an elegant chess set; and one with a brightly colored tarot deck, five cards spread out in some pattern I wasn't familiar with.

Basically, these kids had one expensive playroom. Only problem was, serious money like this also increased the likelihood of them being seriously spoiled brats. But I would wait to judge. My aunt Rhonda had called me a spoiled brat once. That was before Mom died. Now the family rules of civility kept her from saying a word. Didn't stop her from frowning at me like I was an ungrateful pest, though. But her "you're rude" frown was understandable since it usually occurred after I stuck my tongue out at her when my dad wasn't watching.

I contemplated the closed door that separated me from the sleeping twins. Had the last nanny left because they were hard to manage? Would Mr. Pertweath support me ruling my domain? Or were the kids in charge? And if they were, how far would I let them push me? I would have to figure out a way to show them who's boss without getting myself fired. I shrugged. I could handle it. I had to. I pulled Mom's book out of my bag and held it up to my nose. More comfort than made sense in the smell of those worn and yellowed pages.

I touched the looming manor house on the cover. The nanny in Mom's book at first hadn't felt like she belonged, but by the end of the book she had. Could I make this place my home, at least for the summer?

Already I liked the privacy, the way the thick carpet moved under my feet as if I were walking on sand. This place was quiet and soothingly dark.

It felt more like home than Dad's house had lately. I had to face the fact that the house I grew up in wasn't really mine anymore. Krystal's taste had already crept in and taken over. Bright lights and bold colors and furniture without worn spots. She hadn't thought it was funny when I started wearing my shades around the house. But I wasn't kidding. Dad and I had kept things nice and dim after Mom died. I liked it that way, but I guess Dad hadn't, because he smiled a lot more now that the light was back in his life. I was the only one still comfortable with the all-dark look.

I tried to be quiet as I explored, not wanting to wake anyone. My domain turned out to be three rooms, not including whatever was behind the twins' door. Besides the big main room the elevator opened onto, there was a bedroom bigger than the one I had at home and a bathroom with a walk-in shower, a Jacuzzi tub, and one of those fancy art-object sinks made of green glass. The closet was big enough to be a room for a normal person.

I discovered there's nothing that makes you feel poor like seeing your belongings fill up one tenth of the storage space. I arranged my bras, panties, three pairs of jeans, and six tops that Krystal had bought me as a you-got-a-job-and-now-I-don't-have-to-have-you-tag-along-on-my-honeymoon present in the top two drawers of the antique dresser in my room. First I tried spacing them out into all five drawers, but that was more pathetic-looking, so I filled up the top drawers and figured I'd just never open the others—or go into the closet.

I kicked off my sandals and enjoyed the carpet squishing between my toes. Common sense told me I should be sleepy. I wasn't, though. I wanted to soak in the place while it was still dark and quiet and all mine. While I could pretend that there weren't two little girls sleeping one room away, waiting for me to wipe their runny noses and make sure they didn't come to any harm. Here I could pretend, for just a little longer, that my life was a cocoon, and I could curl up in it if I wanted.

It helped that this nanny's bedroom had the four-poster bed I'd wanted since I was ten. I slipped Mom's book under one thick puffy pillow. Teddy Smithers, who's been with me since I was two, I put on the bed with my iPod and cell phone. "Look, Teddy. We have a domain." He seemed impressed.

I heard a soft ding in the big room and went out to see a light blinking on the far wall, by the elevator. It took me a second to figure out how to get the dumbwaiter open, but it was worth it, because there was a covered tray of food, just like room service in a hotel. I lifted the top to find a tuna sandwich and some chips and a big glass of water with ice and lemon in it.

The tuna was delicious and I think the chips were homemade. Best of all, I could eat it without worrying that I'd have to hear Dad yell about the bill when we checked out. I wasn't checking out. I was on the clock. I was getting paid to eat this sandwich and sleep in a four-poster bed. Sarah was going to be so jealous when I told her.

I looked at the kids' closed door. Even if they were terrible brats, I wasn't going to let them get to me. This place was too perfect.

I opened the binder marked "Nanny Notes." There was a glossy brochure about Chrysalis Cliff, so I read as I ate. This place was the twilight zone in more ways than one. The brochure promised elegance, privacy, luxury, and a total karmic transformation for "those looking for a subtle and youth-enhancing nip and tuck of the spirit." There were sessions of yoga and massages of every kind, which seemed to offer people a fast track to finding and fixing their snarled karmic threads.

I wasn't too surprised to read about tarot readings, since the kids had a table. But the séance room gave me a squee moment. It looked like something out of the old black-and-white movies my mom and I used to watch when I stayed home sick from school. Big stone fireplace, round table with thick Victorian legs surrounded by sturdy chairs that didn't look easy to slide around. A chandelier hung over the table like a big fat spider waiting for the next fly.

The "Nanny Notes" were not as rooted in the otherworldly. Apparently, the twins' day ran on a tight schedule. They got up, took their showers, and got dressed by seven thirty. There was no notation as to whether I was supposed to help. Since I would not have wanted help picking out my clothes when I was ten, I decided to err on the side of caution tomorrow and wait for the twins to emerge from their room. If they came out naked, I could readjust my conception of my nanny duties. If not, we were golden. The rest of the schedule was filled with activities such as music lessons, research, reading, meals, aerobic exercise, and "mandatory fun time." There was a parenthetical notation that this was not to be skipped under any circumstance, without prior approval of Mr. Pertweath. Interesting.

I was halfway through the notes and the sandwich, and all the way finished with the chips when I heard a scrabbling, whispery sound. I braced myself, staring at the door to the twins' room. If this were a movie, they'd be plotting to put a snake or a frog in my bed. Or waiting to see how I would react to the one they'd already put there before I even arrived. My best hope was that without TV they hadn't seen the movies about how to torment a nanny.

I watched the doorknob. Was it turning? No. Just the shadows. The whispery rustle continued and then, finally, the doorknob actually turned and the door swung open.

I expected . . . well, I don't really know what I expected. Kids, I guess. Like the ones I'd been babysitting since I turned thirteen.

Instead, two miniature people came out. The kind of people who looked like they hadn't ever been children, even when they'd worn diapers. I don't know how they did it. It wasn't their appearance—their plain black pajamas and sleep-rumpled hair. Maybe it was the way they carried themselves. They didn't peek around the door, just walked out like they owned the place. They didn't have any of that hesitation that kids usually have when they're doing something they might get yelled at for.

The taller twin stuck out her hand. "You must be the new nanny. I'm Rienne."

I wiped the chip grease off my hands with a napkin and shook. "I hope I didn't wake you." I know the formality sounds silly, but, really, they were staring at me so solemnly it was all I could do not to curtsy. "I'm Philippa."

Rienne nodded. "May we call you Pippa?"

Only my Mom had called me that, so the question jolted me a little. "You may, if you like." What the heck, I was taking my life back from Krystalization, why not take my nickname back?

The other twin asked, "So, do you really like black?"

Rienne looked at her sister with a frown. "Triste, don't be frivolous. Look what she's wearing."

"We've been through this before," Triste answered her sister patiently. I had a strange feeling, like I was the child and they the two grown-ups, discussing me as though I could not hear.

"Look at the jeans. I think she hand sewed those silk squares and that lace on the pockets herself." Rienne looked at me and I nodded.

Triste opened her mouth to say something else, but Rienne stopped her. "Look at the jeans, that's great work, and not done yesterday, either, if you were going to suggest it was only done to fit in here."

Triste said with a world-weary sigh, "Excuse me, Pippa. You wouldn't believe how many nanny types there are who like pastels like pink and blue."

Rienne nodded. "Or tan and brown. That's at least sixty percent of the nanny wardrobe."

Triste sat down across the table from me. "True. That's why we specified 'must love black' in the ad. We need a nanny who understands us. The pastel types can't handle the job."

I was a little curious to hear about the previous nanny runaways, but I knew better than to invite them to try to spook me with horror stories. I had been babysitting long enough to know that I had to take the upper hand right away, or I'd be dead nanny walking.

I said, "I always wear black. It's a good color. Sensible. Doesn't show dirt." I stood up and brushed off a few chip crumbs. "Do I send this back down on the dumbwaiter?"

"Yes," they said together. A little creepy. They showed me how. I liked sending the dirty dishes away and forgetting about them. At home a dirty dish in the sink might get me a ten-minute lecture from Krystal.

Then I said, "Time to turn in. We can meet more officially tomorrow." They stared at me without moving.

Great. No way was I going to let them get away with a summer of not listening to me. I walked toward the door to their room. "Do you like to be tucked in?"

Rienne, obviously the chattier twin, shook her head and moved past me through the door. "No, thank you. Although tomorrow night we will expect you to read to us from our bedtime book."

"No problem."

Triste took my hand, I thought she wanted to shake good-bye before she went back to bed, but she turned my hand over and thoughtfully traced the lines on my palm. She turned to her sister. "Just like the handwriting analysis suggested. I think we have a keeper."

CHAPTER FOUR

*You have a responsibility to your children, my lord. A responsibility
to help them be better than you, if you will forgive my boldness.*
—Miss Adelaide Putnam to Lord Dashwood,
Manor of Dark Dreams, p. 22

"What?" I glanced down at my palm. Just a plain palm, still a
tiny bit greasy from the chips. I refocused on the solemn little
girl who was staring at me with enormous—and enormously
sincere—brown eyes.

Rienne nodded, and I could have sworn there was a self-
satisfied "I told you so" lurking in her tone when she said,
"Handwriting analysis is very useful."

Triste apparently noticed the lurking smugness too,
because she frowned a little before she said, "The 'must love
black' line was equally important." I had the feeling that had
been her contribution, and I wasn't sure how I felt knowing
that two ten-year-olds had written the job advertisement for
their new nanny.

Rienne dismissed that contribution. "Maybe, to attract her to apply. But anyone can say they love black, and handwriting is the only way to ensure they're not lying."

Rienne turned to me and said proudly, "We convinced Father that that was the best way to find someone who would be compatible with us."

They looked gravely at each other in some kind of weird twin communication, then at me. "At least for the summer," they said in unison.

Hmm. That was good, right? They wanted me to stay. I guess I didn't have to look for rats or toads. Yet.

I tried to sound firm, though I was no longer sure I needed to. They were a pretty serious pair of kids. "Good night, then. See you in the morning."

"Good night." They shut themselves in their room and I stood there for a moment, just letting what I'd learned about them sink in. After a few minutes, the weight of the day got to me and I decided going to bed was a good idea.

My bed at home was not nearly as nice, but it was mine, centered against the wall with all my posters and the window that looked out on the tree my mom and I had planted one day when the local tree huggers were giving out seedlings. I'd wanted to plant as many as my chubby little hands could hold, but Mom explained that trees needed space and sun to grow big, and it wouldn't be good to crowd them.

There was a window in this room, too. I moved the curtain aside and squinted. Thick fog pressed against the glass.

The window opened smoothly. It didn't have a screen, so I could stick my head out into the fog. It was cool and damp on my face. The quiet of the house was eased by the sound of the sea and the wind.

I climbed into bed, watching the curtains flap in the breeze, wondering what the outside would look like in the daytime, when the fog had burned off. I left the window open but didn't turn my back to it when I curled up.

Teacups, commence your whirling. I flipped the pages of my mother's book with my thumb, enjoying the sound and feel of the page edges too much to stop.

The box that held two dozen copies of Mom's new book came the day of her funeral. I took one to throw in the grave. The funeral director shooed me away, because I was only nine. I'd had to wait until he was turned away, whispering to my Dad, to drop it dead center on the shiny brown casket. For a moment, the woman on the cover seemed to look at me as if she disapproved of being buried alive when all she was trying to do was escape the menace of the dark and brooding stone manor behind her, but then the book slid down the shiny hump of the casket and tucked itself between the sharp wall of dirt and the glossy glorified box.

Mom said once, when I was squishing the soap bubbles up between my fingers carefully so my hands would be clean enough to pat the pages, that a writer puts all her best lines in her first book. That if you read a writer's first book, you'll know who she is. She said that's why a lot of writers can't get their first books published—or don't even try. Because they don't want to edit themselves out, as much as they need to. She said that was silly, because when you edit a lot of yourself out, the best remains and shines through.

Must Love Black   39

I didn't pay attention then because she was my mom and I was just a kid and she was alive. But now I know what she meant. Whenever I'm not sure what to do, I check her book for advice. I've never told anyone this, because it's no one else's business. Besides, it's not like anyone else cares what she had to say in her first and last novel, *Manor of Dark Dreams*. The book came out, Dad and I drove to the store and took pictures in front of it on the bookshelf, and then it disappeared. She was working on another book she called *Manor of Dark Hope*, but it died with her since the only copy was on her laptop, which got destroyed in the crash.

Whenever I need to hear what my mom would have said, I close my eyes and stick my finger somewhere on the page and read. It may sound twisted, but I swear she hasn't ever let me down. She really did put all the best of herself in that book. I'd used it a lot when I was little—right through freshman year, when the advice kept me from betraying Sarah over some guy who was cuter than sin and liked to play girls as if we were stones he could pick up and skip across a pond. He didn't concern himself with the ripples, of course. Still didn't, as of the end of junior year. But Sarah and I had avoided being rippled apart by his electric smile and careless ways.

Close call, though, and I'm not sure I'd have understood the right thing to do if I hadn't read my mom's wise words (page 29, second paragraph):

> Friendship is a choice. More to the point, it is a
> series of ongoing choices, with consequences
> for each person. And thus I decided that I

would not speak of Arabella's hoarding of the dinner rolls. As her nanny I could not precisely be her friend, but neither did I need to be her enemy.

When I finally put aside the book and turned out the light, the day's events made an imprint on my dreams—wedding cake with two tiny twin figures atop the highest tier; Geoff and me driving in the fog, only to find that we weren't on a road any longer; Krystal throwing me her bouquet of roses and me catching a handful of thorny stems.

Just as I dropped the bouquet and saw the blood on my palms spelling out "beware ghosts," I woke to a banging sound. I was so disoriented from my odd dreams that I checked to make sure my palms weren't really bloody. I looked at the window with fear, forgetting for a moment that I was not at home. There was a white wispy face at my window. I lay completely still as my sleepy brain sought to sound the alarm and my reason tried to reassure me that it could not be a face. My room was three floors up. It was only fog.

I closed my eyes and tried to settle back to sleep. But when I opened one eye to double-check the window, the fog face leered at me and moaned a soft and unambiguous, "Helllllp themmmmmm." I sat up with a gasp worthy of any Victorian nanny and instantly felt like an idiot.

The face dissipated as the fog pressed and roiled outside, a dozen faces forming and bleeding away under my sharp gaze.

I sighed, and calmed my racing heart. No ghost. Only fog. I checked my palms, for good measure. No blood. Just dreams. I hugged Teddy Smithers in one arm and *Manor of Dark Dreams* in the other. And then I went back to sleep and refused to dream until daylight woke me.

In Maine, in summer, on the coast, that's really early, about 4:30 a.m. Once the first rays of the morning entered my room, I couldn't get back to sleep. I picked up my phone and debated whether to call Sarah. Call her early or wait? If I called now, I would definitely be waking her up. But if I waited, I might miss my chance. Her family was supposed to leave that morning on their Habitat for Humanity trip, and once they left, Sarah would become much harder to reach. She had a phone in her bedroom, but she didn't own a cell. After finding that my phone got a signal only when I stood at my bedroom window (sure enough, it had a gorgeous ocean view), I opted to call now and later beg her forgiveness for waking her up. She answered a little sleepily, but then her voice brightened. "How'd it go with Geoff?"

"Got any tips for getting a guy to talk? He takes 'man of few words' to a whole new level."

She sighed, and I could hear her finger tapping as she thought for a minute. "Ask open-ended questions that he can't answer with yes or no."

"Tried that. Anything else?"

She laughed. "Count yourself lucky he's good-looking and stop pushing for more than that?"

"Thanks a lot."

"Seriously. You know you're bad about wanting perfect-perfect. Take the summer off and accept a little loosening of those famous Philippa standards, why don't you."

"Easy for you to say," I grumped.

"Hey! I let the standards fall every summer—some of those guys can't even hit a nail straight, but if they're cute or funny, I'm not complaining. Just go with it."

The spinning sensation in my chest stopped at the idea of just accepting Geoff as he was for the summer. The kids, too. I gazed out at the ocean. Maybe it was time to try a change from the inside out. After all, it was only three months. I could do anything for three months.

All too soon Sarah had to hang up and join the family trek to do-gooderville. I stared at the phone in my hand, wondering how often we'd get to talk with me busy working here and Sarah busy working on a Habitat for Humanity site.

She had promised to try to beg a cell phone from someone to call me once in a while. I was sure it wouldn't happen often, though.

I made my great four-poster all neat, just like I hadn't slept in it. I never made my bed at home, but it just seemed right to do it here. I liked the way the room looked so perfect again, just like a dream room for a girl whose life was perfect. You know, the two-loving-parents, no-icky-stepmother kind of girl.

My bathroom had a shower with six jets. Six! After a few false starts where I sprayed cold water directly into my face, I figured it out and stayed in there for at least half an hour with no sign of the hot water running out. Sarah was going to be so jealous when I told her.

Part of me was enjoying the luxury; part of me felt like the cops were going to burst in and arrest me for so obviously not belonging in this place. It didn't seem right that the nanny had a room this amazing. I wondered what the twins' room looked like.

There was a coffeepot in the bathroom. One of those fancy machines that makes one cup, fast. I made myself a cup of the Brazilian roast. New day, new life. The coffee was good, especially when I poked around under the smooth green granite countertop and found a minifridge with organic half-and-half and a few containers of yogurt and bottles of juice. There was a note, too, that said, "Miss, please enjoy these and order replacements from the kitchen when required—Havens." How weird. He signed his name "Havens." Did he have a first name? I bet it would be something like Sebastian or Charles or maybe Frederick like the butler in Mom's book.

When I went out into the common room, fortifying mug of coffee in hand, Triste and Rienne were already there. Apparently, late-night meetings with the new nanny didn't make them want to sleep late.

They were dressed, both mostly in black. I noticed that Triste had tried to do the layer thing like I had worn last night. I don't think this was normal for her, though, because she'd done it all wrong, putting a bulky layer on the top and totally messing up the lighter layer underneath. Not that I had any intention of correcting her. Clearly, she was smart. She'd figure it out. In my experience, people who liked black didn't like being told that they hadn't quite gotten the hang of something yet. Better to figure it out on your own.

There was a big tray with bowls and a pitcher of milk and a

pot of something hot on the round table. The binder had been pushed aside to make room. I looked in the pot. Oatmeal. With a bowl of fresh blueberries next to it. There's really nothing like fresh Maine blueberries, small, full of tart flavor, and not at all mealy. Oatmeal seemed a little retrocentury, but I was hungry. I put a little in a bowl and sat down.

"Why don't you have breakfast downstairs with your dad?" It could be tricky asking them questions about the way the house was run. But I'd rather ask a pair of ten-year-olds than the butler—or even Geoff.

"He's very busy," Triste answered as she lined her blueberries on top of her oatmeal in a checkered pattern.

Rienne nodded. Her blueberries were in a swirl pattern, except where she'd dug in for her first bite of oatmeal. "He used to run the business with our mother, but now that she's gone he has to do it alone."

Triste added, "He just got a new partner, and she is very demanding of his time."

"A new partner?" She? Maybe I was oversensitive, but it sounded like the twins were on the way to joining me in stepmotherland. "I guess running this place is a lot for one person."

Rienne said, "Besides the yoga instructors and meditation counselors and masseuses for the guests, we have a staff of six: Ginger, the cook; Havens, the butler; Geoff, the gardener; Graciela, the housekeeper; Lionel, the chauffeur; and Laurie, the personal assistant."

Triste shook her head. "Seven. Don't forget Pippa. She's staff too."

Rienne argued, "But she doesn't help keep this place running smoothly for the guests, now, does she?"

I didn't quite like being low on the staff totem pole. "I get the most important job," I told them.

"What's that?" they both asked at the same time, staring at me with identical gazes.

I'd only meant it as a joke, but their grave eyes made my voice more serious. "Taking care of you, of course. I'm sure your dad thinks that's more important than running a business, don't you?" Okay, so I didn't really think that, but I felt for the kids, especially if their dad's new partner was going to end up being their new mother. Let them think they mattered to him. For a little while longer. From the smiles on their faces, it seemed my strategy worked.

I decided to change the subject. "So, you guys are into computers, are you?" This may have been a complete under-statement given the four huge monitors that dominated one side of the room. The twins had already turned them on, and the room had an electronic hum going on. It was interesting that a father who banned television and radio still indulged this obsession. Or maybe computers were an interest they'd shared with their mother.

"We do our research and studies on the Internet," Rienne explained.

"I'm surprised your dad lets computers in the house, if he bans TV." I said it casually, as if I didn't mind the lack of a television. Fortunately, summer was rerun season, so I wasn't missing too much.

"Computers are nothing like TV," said Triste.

Rienne argued, "They can be, but we don't use our computers for mindless entertainment. We use them for education."

Education? Was I supposed to teach them during the day? I thought about what I could teach them, and came up with two things: how to make store-bought jeans look fashionable and how to write poetry. I'm a good poet, so my teachers say. But the thought of showing these two minipeople my poems was intimidating. They would argue about my word choice, my meter, my rhyme. Maybe not my subject matter—after all, they liked black as much as I did. Still, I'd rather not do a show-and-tell my first morning.

Which left me wondering what exactly I was supposed to do. It was probably written somewhere in the binder, along with the daily schedule, but it seemed weird to open that in front of them and consult it. I considered asking them directly, but it didn't seem very nannylike. I'd gotten into big trouble that way once while babysitting—I'd asked a kid what snacks his mom let him have. He'd told me peanut butter crackers. It wasn't until after he started swelling up that he admitted he had an allergy and showed me the EpiPen.

I tried a compromise question. "So, what are you working on right now?"

They took me over to the computer and started talking about something they called "Camp CSI." Apparently, it was an online camp that gave children a chance to do their own CSI-type experiments. Even though the twins didn't watch TV, they understood investigative procedures and were fascinated by the camp.

Rienne tapped a few keys and showed me their mission for today: take pictures of a butterfly and then figure out what kind of butterfly it is using the butterfly files in the "camp library."

Triste frowned. "It's not the most challenging mission for us because of the butterfly garden." She didn't seem to like taking the easy way.

Rienne shook her head. "The hard part isn't taking a picture of the butterfly, Triste, it's identifying it. That won't be easy."

Triste nodded thoughtfully. "I suppose you're right. But let's take a picture of a butterfly that's really different from the rest, to make it a little bit harder."

Rienne shrugged. "Okay. If you want."

Watching them talk about their mission with such confidence, I let my attention wander to another computer and wondered if I could use it for e-mail. Sarah had said she'd check her e-mail. And so had Dad.

I had just sat down to check my e-mail when an old-fashioned bong sounded from somewhere in the ceiling. I looked up. The twins didn't move, so neither did I.

When the bong sounded a second time, Triste sighed. "You're being paged, Pippa."

"By the ceiling?" I looked around.

"Here." Rienne leaned over the computer terminal, clicked on a desktop icon, and suddenly, Havens's face filled my monitor. A little scary, even though he'd seemed fairly harmless last night. "Good morning, Miss. Good morning, children. I trust you all slept well and enjoyed your breakfast."

"Yes, we did." Since I could see him, I assumed he could see me, so I sat a little straighter and tried to look like a responsible nanny who has everything under control.

"Mr. Pertweath would like to speak with you before you begin today, Miss."

"No problem." Maybe he'd clue me in on what I was supposed to do.

"He's scheduled fifteen minutes for you—his day's rather busy, you understand. If you could be downstairs in ten minutes, I'll meet you at the elevator and show you to his office."

"I'll be there."

"Excellent."

Havens's face disappeared from the monitor.

"He always calls the nannies 'Miss.' Isn't that a funny thing?" Rienne said.

"Sounds nice to me." I shrugged.

"It's just because he can't bother to remember your name," Triste informed me.

I ignored this comment. "I should have asked if you were supposed to come with." I looked at the monitor. It seemed likely that I could page Havens if he could page me, but I didn't have a clue how, and I didn't want to admit that to the twins.

Fortunately, Rienne piped up, "Oh, no. We're going for our music lesson at eight thirty."

Right. I remembered seeing that on the schedule.

"Am I supposed to take you?" Technically, I was able to drive. Not that I'd done much of it. It's not that I didn't enjoy driving, it's just that I didn't trust the other drivers on the road not to make stupid mistakes that could get me into an accident. Hey, it happens.

Before the twins could answer, the elevator door slid open and a very pretty young woman emerged. I pinpointed her as Laurie, the personal assistant, since she looked too young to be Mr. Pertweath's business partner, and her blazer, heels, and skirt seemed too formal for a cook. She wasn't more than two or three years older than I was, at most.

"Who's ready to go for music lessons?" She was a little on the peppy and pink side of life for me. Especially this early in the morning.

Apparently the twins agreed because they groaned and said in unison, "Laurie, you don't have to pretend we're not doing this under protest."

"Hey, Lionel's still off today, so you get to spend some quality time with Geoff. You can't tell me you mind that."

"He is cute," Triste agreed. Rienne nodded. I tried to size up Laurie without being too obvious about it. Sounded like she thought Geoff was cute too. I wondered if she knew if he was taken.

"See? There's always an upside." Laurie was way too cheery. I wondered if she had a quirky side, like Sarah. I'm not much for instabonding with summer friends, but it could be cool to have a girl around my age to hang out with, and she might have the scoop on Geoff. But then she wagged her finger at the girls. "Just so long as you don't get any ideas about my guy."

CHAPTER FIVE

There was no sense longing for the man. He was as far out of my reach as the moon.
　　　—Miss Adelaide Putnam, *Manor of Dark Dreams*, p. 25

Her guy? Geoff was taken? Bummer. Not that I'd planned to make a move on him, not without Sarah to egg me on, but Geoff, taciturn and hot, had presented a bit of a challenge. I like a challenge. Maybe I didn't want to date him, but I had hoped to get him to say more than one sentence in a row. I looked at Laurie and realized that trying to do so would definitely be a waste. If Geoff liked this pink-and-pretty, bubble-gum couture-suit wearer, then he and I didn't have enough in common for me to be interested in hearing more than one sentence from him.

We all took the elevator down to the main floor, where Havens met me. I had hoped to see Geoff there, too. Just to see if he was as into Laurie as she sounded like she was into him. After all, I believe in a fair trial with all facts and evidence on the table before I condemn someone to loserdom. No go, though. Laurie and the twins peeled off toward what I assumed was the direction of the garage while I followed Havens through the smooth and shiny marble hallway where he'd welcomed me last night.

The house seemed to grow bigger and bigger—the meditation center, a yoga wing, a Pilates studio. We wended our way past two conference rooms and a bank of private elevators that each led to a different guest suite. Finally, Havens and I stepped into a sunlit lobby where patrons check in and out, and then into a hushed office with some woo-woo music playing very low and the faintest hint of incense in the air. I glanced with curiosity at the elegant and paper-laden desk Havens identified as Laurie's. She wasn't much older than I was and she was working as Mr. Pertweath's personal assistant.

Havens touched a red button on Laurie's phone and a voice came over the intercom, drowning out the music on the sound system: "Perfect timing, Havens. Send her in."

I stepped through the double doors that Havens held open, into an office as big as the entire first floor of the house I'd grown up in. The woo-woo music wasn't playing in here, but the scent of incense was a little stronger. There was a massive and ornate desk with curved legs and carved detail that I wasn't close enough to make out. There was no one at the desk, so I looked around.

"Welcome, Miss Munson. Philippa." The man who had spoken was sitting on a yoga mat in front of a marble fireplace. He sat easily in the lotus position and I felt a twinge of envy. When we'd learned yoga in gym class, I'd barely been able to do a half lotus. Of course, that had been in a gym, and this was in an office.

Mr. Pertweath gestured to a low chair near his mat. "Please sit. Let's chat a bit about the girls and your duties."

He wasn't at all what I had expected. The girls had said he was busy, but where were the piles of papers? The phone ringing off the hook? I sat on the edge of the chair, my nerves strung tightly like the strings of a violin. He, unnervingly, seemed perfectly relaxed, and he even smiled. It was in direct contrast to his daughters, who didn't seem able to relax or smile. Which was why it surprised me when he said, "We're so happy to have you here. I think you're just what the girls need to have fun this summer."

When I think of dads, I think of mine—or at least the way mine used to be. You know, the kind of guy who wants his kids to do well but isn't quite sure what the definition of "do well" is. But I don't think it ever includes a blanket mandate to "have fun."

So I guess I can be forgiven for blinking in dull surprise when he said, "A young person is closer to the concept of fun, don't you think?"

"Sure." Of course I didn't think that, not if the young person had been attracted by an ad that said "must love black." But I wasn't going to say so to my new boss. At least, not until I'd figured him out and had an idea of what might get me fired. I didn't intend to run away from the job, and I certainly didn't intend to get booted out, either. So I said cautiously, "But the twins don't really seem that into fun."

"Ah." He nodded thoughtfully. "They've had a bad year.

Lost their mother, you know." He pointed to the portrait hanging over the fireplace behind him. A family portrait with a woman as unsmilingly serious as her children and a man who smiled proudly as if he didn't notice the solemn expressions of his wife and daughters. "Your job is to remind them that fun is not a four-letter word. I expect you to see to it that Rienne and Triste experience fun daily, as called for on their schedule. They take things far too seriously. A little fun is exactly what they need to get over that."

Now, I'd met the twins. "Fun" didn't seem to be in their vocabulary. And the portrait suggested they'd felt that way before their mother died. Shouldn't their father already know that? I probably shouldn't have spoken my mind, but I did: "I don't think they can be forced to have fun if they're not ready. Wouldn't you agree?"

"Forced?" He looked horrified at the word. "Of course not. I was thinking cajoled, enticed, maybe pushed just a little." He grinned at me, and I realized the man did know a little bit about cajoling, for sure. But he seemed more clueless than conniving when it came to his daughters.

"Philippa, they're children. All children want to have fun. No matter what they say."

I knew better than to tell him what I really thought. What I knew. Happy sneaks up on you even in the worst of times. Screeching of metal on metal, crash of glass, and boom, you're hurt. But then you see Teddy Smithers made it through unscathed and a little bubble of happiness comes from behind the headache forming at the base of a bounced-around skull. Until you notice the next bad thing—your mom isn't moving. Happy is like cotton candy—sweet and so full of air it disappears before you swallow.

"You're the nanny. You know best. They're the children. They'll listen to you." He stiffened when the grandfather clock behind his desk began to chime the hour.

Before he or I could say another word, a woman burst into the room. She was dressed like a cross between a Greek goddess and a space alien—in some kind of shiny, soft silver wraparound garment that wafted gracefully around her when she moved but didn't get in the way or slow down her charge toward what she wanted. Which, at the moment, appeared to be Mr. Pertweath.

He leaped up, flushing guiltily. The Zen calm was completely gone. "Lady Buena Verde." I realized who she was at the same moment. She didn't look anything like the woman in the itsy bitsy headshot I'd seen in the brochure last night. The new partner. I realized I'd been wrong about the stepmother angle. She was old enough to be Mr. P's mother and the twins' grandmother. But I was right about her charging in like Krystal and changing everything about their lives.

She looked at him as if he were five. "Mr. Pertweath, you're making your guest wait."

"I'm so sorry." He looked at her, then at me. I wasn't sure who he was apologizing to. Maybe the universe, because he also checked out the ceiling briefly. "The new nanny, you know. Very important."

"Of course. Important." Lady Buena Verde glanced at me as if I was anything but important. "But rather simple to dispatch in fifteen minutes, as scheduled, yes? Now go change. You certainly can't meet our most important patron in yoga gear."

I was frozen at the edge of the chair, watching for my chance to escape. No luck. Lady BV (as I was already calling her in my head) turned her energy force on me. "Welcome, child."

I took the opportunity to stand up and take a step toward the door. Before I could move past her, she grabbed my hand in both of hers. "So glad that you've signed on to take the twins in hand. You know they are to remain out of the guests' way, of course, but—" she broke off. "My goodness . . ." Lady BV turned my palm up and stared down at it with a puzzled frown.

I pulled away. "Nice to meet you," I lied. I'd already been honest enough for one morning. Not that it had gotten me anywhere.

"Oh, my." She raised her hands to her temples and absently massaged them as she stared at me with very sharp green eyes. "I sense sadness. Despair."

I shoved my hand into my pocket. "I'm fine." I looked at Mr. Pertweath, who hadn't moved to change his clothes. Apparently he was as paralyzed by Lady Buena Verde as I was. "Ready to have fun, fun, fun."

Mr. P smiled, unfreezing. "Excellent. I knew it wasn't a mistake to hire someone so young. No time for life to have jaded you." I let him hurry off through a small door in the corner of his office. No need to enlighten him about the reason I loved black. For smaller children, grown-ups are a puzzle without all the pieces, a solution that is shrouded in the space between understanding that what is said is not always what is meant. "Eat your vegetables" may mean "Hush and let me eat in peace" or "You must be healthy and obedient or I'll look bad."

I wasn't a little kid anymore; I knew Mr. Pertweath's sentence really meant that he was glad I wasn't old enough to argue with him.

So many meanings hide in the breaths between sentences. I'd learned a long time ago that it was better to be quiet enough to hear those breaths, and thoughtful enough to reconcile words, pauses, actions, and reality in the moment of speech. My bad habits of impatience and unwelcome honesty sometimes got in the way. I wanted to tame them. I knew way too well that being honest about what isn't being spoken aloud is more dangerous than not noticing the gap between words and meaning.

Right. Not that I would say so.

Lady Buena Verde's sharp gaze became unfocused as she stared at me, and her voice softened and slurred ever so slightly. "Your aura . . . so tinged with black. I can help you."

"That's kind of you, but I'm here to provide help, not receive it."

"But—"

"I love black. That's why I was hired."

She looked confused, maybe because Mr. Pertweath didn't clue her in about the ad his daughters had written. I was saved from having to explain when Laurie popped through the double doors at the same moment that Mr. Pertweath reappeared looking like a company director instead of a yoga instructor. Laurie tapped the Blackberry in her hand, a frown on her face. "We're due in the private reading room. Is something the matter?" She looked at me as if I was the cause of the problem.

Mr. Pertweath smiled at me absently and took Lady Buena Verde's arm, breaking her trance. "Laurie, please see that Philippa has whatever she needs for the children, will you? Philippa, I look forward to a full report on the progress of the fun."

And then he and Lady Buena Verde were gone.

I shook my head, still processing the last twenty minutes. "He wants me to force the kids to have fun."

Laurie nodded as if this was a perfectly natural request. "I believe there's a ball in the storage room. Perhaps we could arrange some kind of game in the outer field?"

"The outer field?" How much property was there at Chrysalis Cliff?

"Well, I suppose the tennis courts might be better, but they're reserved for the patrons during daylight hours, and I don't think the children should be playing tennis at night, do you? And the inner field is similarly reserved." She looked at me, with her perfectly plucked eyebrows raised in faint horror. "You have read the schedule, haven't you?"

"Of course," I lied. "And Lady Buena Verde was very clear that the children are not to interfere with the guests' enjoyment."

"Good. That's very important. There was a nanny who just refused to understand, and we had to let her go." Laurie smiled. "So, should I instruct Geoff to find the ball and make sure the outer field is clear of debris so the children can enjoy a game of dodgeball?"

Dodgeball? I guess my skepticism was written on my face, because she quickly added, "I could play too. And I know I could convince Geoff to play with us, for me. It could be Geoff and me against you and the twins."

Lovely. She was so comfortable planning Geoff's day that I wanted to barf. "I'll ask the twins." I wasn't lying, I was just skipping some critical information. I would ask the twins—on my last day here. No way was I going to play dodgeball. Dodgeball can be war or play, depending on the nature of your heart—soft heart and the ball strikes with a mushy thump, hard heart and the ball bounces with an extra edge.

No way was I getting myself in Laurie's crosshairs in a game where winner takes all and grinds the others into the dirt. If I had to force the girls to have Mr. Pertweath's kind of fun, I'd at least have to identify an activity that we could get through alive.

Swimming, maybe. My year on the swim team had taught me that repetitive exercise submerged in a pool can shrivel the fingers and toes and senses—or free someone from the weight of grieving and allow the grounded to fly. The twins were definitely grounded, as I noticed when they filed back in from their music lesson and refused to talk about what they had learned, if anything.

I didn't push it. Music could be fun, but it sounded like the twins didn't find it enjoyable. I didn't see how I could turn it into fun retroactively. So I concentrated on what I could do: help them get the butterfly pictures they needed for Camp CSI. It wouldn't count toward fun in Mr. Pertweath's book, but it was what the twins wanted to do. And if the butterfly garden was as good for spotting gardeners as it was for spotting butterflies . . . well, then checking it out was what I wanted too.

CHAPTER SIX

Life in other people's houses, by other people's rules, can be quite unexceptional—until your own values charge you with one duty while the household rules bring you up short of that duty. Then, a life of sufferance is no different from a choke collar for a disobedient dog.
—Miss Adelaide Putnam to Daisy, the chambermaid,
Manor of Dark Dreams, p. 52

Back in our domain the twins gathered their camera and tripod for our foray into the wilds of the butterfly garden. I was curious to see what it looked like. I'd never heard of such a thing, which underscored the difference between these kids and me: They lived in a world I couldn't comprehend.

Triste grabbed two pairs of binoculars, which struck me as curious. Did you have to hunt butterflies from afar? Weren't they just there, flitting around on the flowers?

I quickly looked at the Nanny Notes binder to make sure our butterfly expedition wouldn't break any rules. Lady Buena Verde had been clear on the most important rule: Keep the girls out of the way of the patrons. But the garden wasn't explicitly off-limits, and it didn't seem disruptive to go down and take some quick shots. We walked quietly through the wide marble hallways, past modern sculptures and exotic flower arrangements on antique tables that were scattered here and there.

We didn't see anyone else, and as the girls led me through the maze of the house with the skill of veteran housebreakers, I started to relax. I might not know the drill, but they did.

We paused at a window in the conservatory and scoped out the butterfly garden below. The sight took my breath away, but I didn't let on to the twins. I was the nanny, not the ninny who oohed and aahed over a garden designed to attract butterflies.

As we stood at the window, we heard voices in the hallway. A quiet murmur, perhaps of a spa patron. Then the voice of Lady Buena Verde, clear in her command. "Now I'll drop you off at the sauna for a wonderful refresher after that grueling tarot session." The patrons and Lady BV passed the entry to the conservatory without looking toward us just as Lady Buena Verde declared, "Chrysalis Cliff is committed to helping you improve your mind, spirit, and body. Our staff is top quality. Ask for anything you need. Enjoy yourselves, ladies."

I tensed, but the voices faded and the danger passed in a second. I looked at the girls. They were holding hands and biting their lips. I raised an eyebrow, as if the close call hadn't rattled me as much as it had them. "Next time we should wear camouflage and paint those cool black smears under our eyes."

"Good idea." Triste didn't smile. Did she know I was joking?

Rienne cleared that up. "I think we'd stand out more in camouflage, don't you?" Neither of them knew I was joking.

Oh well. If you have to explain a joke, it doesn't work. I moved forward with our plan. "All clear. We're going to be quiet, quick, and thorough, right? We get our photos and we get out."

They whispered, "Yes, Pippa. Quick and quiet."

We found quite a few butterflies in the garden, fluttering and flitting like butterflies do. White ones, blue ones, brown ones, huge yellow-and-black ones. It felt a little like a fairy-land, to be honest. I'd never seen so many butterflies in my life. Not real ones, anyway. Mom had indulged my preaccident butterfly mania with necklaces, rings, barrettes, and printed sweatshirts. I knew if she'd heard of butterfly gardens, she'd have taken me to one. I wished I could show her this one.

I let the twins wander and argue in fierce whispers about which butterfly was the rarest, while I looked for a black butterfly. I didn't really have a lot of hope of finding one. But it couldn't hurt to look. After all, I was in a butterfly garden.

Triste very quickly found the butterfly she wanted to photograph. "This one," she said as, camera in hand, she softly crept up on the unsuspecting butterfly. It was not the prettiest of the bunch, but she liked it.

Just as she snapped the first picture, Geoff came around the corner carrying pruning shears. He had on a clean T-shirt imprinted with the Chrysalis Cliff logo and a neat pair of jeans. Much better on the eyes than the chauffeur's uniform from yesterday.

He said sternly, "What are you three doing here?"

Even though he smiled and clearly was not serious, the twins backed up and put their hands behind their backs. You'd think he'd found them pulling wings off butterflies rather than innocently photographing them.

I motioned to Triste, who had gotten as still as a baby rabbit sensing a nearby fox, to keep snapping while I defended them. "The girls need some pictures of butterflies for their online camp. We're just going to take a few pictures and then we'll go back upstairs." It seemed reasonable to me.

Geoff nodded. "Don't let me bother you." He started trimming a dead-looking plant and I tried hard not to stare at the way his biceps flexed when he brought the handles of the shears together. Sarah would have made a flirtatious comment, but all I could think about was that Laurie had called him "my guy." What a waste of hotness.

I didn't have a lot of time to enjoy the view, because Lady Buena Verde appeared out of nowhere. She did not look happy. "You can't be here. You must go up." When we didn't move, she shooed us with fluttery hands. "The rules really must be obeyed, Philippa."

I looked at the girls, who were watching Lady Buena Verde with solemn expressions and clutching each other's hand again. Another one of my inconvenient traits surfaced: stubbornness. I knew I would be risking my job if I defied Lady Buena Verde, but it wasn't fair. We couldn't just leave. Rienne didn't have her butterfly picture yet. And as far as I could see, we weren't even close to being in danger of disturbing any guests.

I felt as if roots were growing from my heels into the

ground, which was a very bad sign that my stubborn streak was about to go nuclear. I took a deep breath and looked at the girls. I knew what I wanted to say. And I knew it was going to get me in trouble. I opened my mouth and dug in my heels as a mostly gray butterfly lighted on Lady Buena Verde's head. It fluttered gray wings for a moment, and then took off.

She didn't notice, but the roots in my heels disappeared and I no longer had the urge to argue with Lady Buena Verde. Somehow the butterfly had reminded me that I could opt for the middle path. "We'll wrap things right up, then," I said sweetly but firmly and nodded at Rienne, who took my hint and quickly snapped shots of a few random butterflies. I grabbed the other camera from Triste and took a picture of the mostly gray butterfly that had landed on Lady BV's head. It wasn't the black butterfly I'd been looking for, but it had saved me from losing my job.

Within seconds we were ready to go. I had managed to keep the peace and get us what we needed. I rocked at the nanny job. I grabbed the tripod and led the twins past Lady Buena Verde and back toward the safety and invisibility of our domain.

Geoff had his back to Lady Buena Verde and seemed not to have noticed that we were being shooed out of the garden. But when we scuttled past him, I heard him whisper, "Good work, Philippa. Don't take her on head-to-head, or you'll lose."

I almost stopped, but Lady Buena Verde's glare kept me moving. I didn't need to cause trouble for a guy who might turn out to be my only ally.

Once we were out of the garden, the twins began to

whisper furiously again. "That wasn't fair. Father never would have shooed us out of there," Triste said.

"I don't like her."

"Mother wouldn't like her either."

"You shouldn't say that."

"Why not? It's true. Mother wanted Father to make Chrysalis Cliff more about peace and welcoming."

Interesting.

We scooted back through the house. As we passed the turnoff to Laurie's office, Triste stopped in the middle of the hall. "We should see Father about this."

Rienne stopped, too, but her glance toward Laurie's office didn't look very certain. "What would we say?"

How about "let me out of this prison and be a normal kid if you so badly want me to have fun"? Not that I thought it would be wise to put those words in the twins' mouths.

Triste wasn't so reticent. "We should ask if we can be permitted to photograph butterflies if we need to, and if we behave ourselves, of course."

"Excellent point, Triste." I decided it was time to put on my nanny hat. "We should get permission ahead of time, so we don't feel unfairly scolded in the future." I had a feeling Lady Buena Verde wouldn't be happy, but she wouldn't know until after we'd dealt with the permission issue and cut out her objection.

Laurie was at her desk. A guy was bent over her pointing out something in a newspaper they were both looking at on her desk. For a second I hoped she'd found a new guy, but then they saw us and she jumped up and said, "Philippa, I want you to meet my brother, David."

"Hi," I said, suppressing my disappointment. Her brother. Bummer.

Or not. He straightened up, taking the paper and folding it under his arm as he smiled. "Philippa. What an old-fashioned name." His blue eyes were bright, and I was a little surprised to find myself being checked out with enough interest to make my temperature begin to rise. "I like it."

Triste and Rienne had no time or patience for my flirtation, however. Triste spoke up firmly. "Laurie, we need to see Father."

"You do?" She spoke to them with a lilting tone that made it seem as if she thought they were three, not ten. She patted her brother on the arm and gave him a no-nonsense sisterly look that said "get lost." "I guess we can talk more about this at home, okay?"

He nodded and threw me a rueful smile as he left. I wondered if he came by often or if this was a rare treat, but I didn't know how to ask. Not that it would matter since we weren't allowed to leave our domain.

"So, what exactly is the problem?" Laurie asked. If the twins wanted to see their father, they would first have to get past his gatekeeper.

Rienne told Laurie our plight and she dropped her jaw in shock. "You didn't!"

Great. Everyone here thought it was okay for the girls to be locked away like freaks. I said, "Well, yes, I'm afraid we did."

Laurie picked up her Blackberry and pushed a few buttons. "Lady Buena Verde saw you?"

Was that really the most important question? "Sure. But

she didn't turn into dust or melt away, so don't worry."

"Oh, no!" Laurie cried.

I could feel the girls getting more and more tense at the idea that they'd broken some big rule. Laurie was totally channeling Lady BV, treating them like inconvenient obstacles to business. Well, Laurie and Lady Buena Verde might have been happy to lock the kids in a tower, but I was under explicit instructions from Mr. Pertweath himself to make sure that his daughters got a daily dose of fun. "What's the big deal?" I blurted.

Laurie gave me an awfully patronizing look for someone who was basically my age. "Guests pay for peace and quiet. Frolicking children are not peaceful or quiet."

I glanced at the twins. Were we talking about the same kids? "We weren't frolicking. We were quietly taking pictures in the butterfly garden."

Laurie's tone softened. "I guess you can be forgiven. This time. But you have to understand that we run on very carefully arranged schedules. There are people here who don't want to see another soul but Lady Buena Verde—not patron, staff, or interloper. They pay good money for that privilege. I hope you understand."

"I guess." I thought about it for a minute. Solitude in a house full of people. Yeah, I could see why it would be worth a lot of money.

"Well, I suppose no harm was done." Laurie looked at the twins.

Triste spoke up. "We'd really like to see Father. Just for three minutes."

"I'm sorry, girls, your father is in private sessions all afternoon," Laurie sing-songed. Then she turned to me sternly. "From now on, please stick to the schedule. That's why you were hired, you know."

I really didn't like being lectured to by someone only a few years older than me. Actually, I didn't like being lectured to at all, by anyone, of any age. But she had me with the job thing. Sigh. "Okay. We'll stick to the schedule." At least until I could get Mr. Pertweath to change it.

Once we were back in our domain, the twins settled at the computers to begin identifying their butterflies. I picked up the binder intending to commit the schedule to heart—both so we wouldn't get in trouble and so I could discuss what should be changed with Mr. Pertweath the next time I saw him. Which, according to the schedule, would be at dinner tonight.

The computer beeped softly, and I felt like I was really beginning to understand the way this place was run as I went to answer Havens's summons.

"Good day, Miss." Havens didn't look too happy. "I'm afraid we have to cancel the family dinner this evening."

"Cancel? No." Triste and Rienne were heartbroken, butterflies forgotten as they came up behind me to see Havens's face on the monitor.

"I'm sorry, girls. Your father's schedule requires it." Havens smiled grimly. "I will send up hot fudge sundaes with your dinner."

"With sprinkles?" Triste asked.

"And whipped cream," Rienne ordered. Then she said

to me, "We always get sundaes if Father has to cancel."

"How nice." Nothing says I love you like a bribe from an absentee parent.

"Would you like one, Miss?" Havens asked.

"Do you have chocolate ice cream?"

"We do."

"Then yes, Havens. I would. Thank you." The simple life. Ask for a hot fudge sundae with chocolate ice cream and ye shall receive through the miracle of a dumbwaiter. I could get spoiled by this life.

"You're welcome, Miss. Girls."

I looked around the room. We got ice cream sundaes, but not freedom. This whole "domain" thing was rapidly beginning to feel like another word for "prison." The doors were fancy, but locked, all the same.

I looked at Rienne and Triste, who'd gone back to identifying butterflies, and felt a stab of sadness. I was choosing to be here, and being paid well for my time—this was a summer job, after all—but they had to live here for at least another eight years, being ignored by their father and lectured to by everyone else. And to think I'd been afraid they might be spoiled brats.

I could see what my most important duty was—and it wasn't on the schedule, naturally. I had to get Mr. P to start making time for his daughters. They needed *him*, not fun. How to convince him of that? Not a clue.

CHAPTER SEVEN

It was my duty to protect the children. It was my heartbreak to have to protect them from their own father's indifferent regard.
—Miss Adelaide Putnam to Lord Dashwood,
Manor of Dark Dreams, p. 22

The next few days were subdued and uneventful. The girls and I stuck to the precious schedule ("dinner in family dining room" was not part of it), and they kept busy doing Internet research on butterflies.

They were enjoying their research, so I did not interrupt it to force them to have "fun," but I knew I would have to cajole them into some other kinds of activities soon, or I would have nothing to report back to Mr. P when he asked how the fun was going. Figuring out a "fun" activity that wouldn't make them miserable was proving as hard as I'd expected. If I were a pastel nanny or a nanny in tan, I might have just pulled out the dolls or the dodgeball ball and forced the twins to play along. But I wasn't that kind of nanny—I was a nanny who loves black—so I wasn't going to force that kind of summer on them. Or on me.

As I watched Triste and Rienne doing their research I felt a certain awe at how self-contained they were. They didn't seem to have any doubts about what they were doing or how they would accomplish their goal. I'd only known them for a few days, but I had a feeling I knew exactly what their response would be to the idea of planning fun: a big fat "Why?"

I decided to make a list of everything the characters in the many books I'd read had considered fun. (I didn't count Tom Sawyer's fence painting.) It wasn't a short list, but I suspected that the girls would very quickly whittle it down to nothing if I allowed them any veto power. Some things were typical summer "fun" things, such as swimming, going to the zoo, and having a bonfire on the beach. Some things were more educational, such as learning to dance or paint or make jewelry. There were some things that wouldn't go well with the be-unseen-and-unheard rule. I starred those.

After the girls went to bed I took my list and a yogurt from my little fridge to bed with me. Sarah hadn't e-mailed or called since that first morning when we'd talked, which wasn't a big surprise; she was probably bonding with her parents on the long drive south. They liked to play the alphabet game and the license plate game when they traveled. Gag me.

Even though it hadn't been foggy since my first night at Chrysalis Cliff, I'd been electing to sleep with my window closed and the curtains pulled. I didn't need any more ghosts visiting me.

By the time I'd made my morning cup of coffee the next

day, I had decided how I would approach the subject of fun with the girls. My brainstorm had come from my dreams. No ghosts, no weddings, just my dad and me at the rail of a whale boat, watching the shore grow tiny as we chugged out on the ocean to catch sight of whales.

My dream had reminded me that pre-Krystal my dad and I used to go to Bar Harbor whenever we couldn't bear to stay in the house. One of us would get that restless feeling and say, "I wonder if the ocean's still there?" It was a question I'd asked as a kid, and Mom and Dad always teased me about it long after I understood that the sea comes back on the tide. Surely Triste and Rienne, cooped up as they were, had to feel a bit of that restlessness? It was only day four for me, and I already did. Maybe if I bribed them with the promise of ice cream cones in town, they would come along and fall into having fun without even realizing it.

I looked at the twins, hunched over their cereal bowls, reading. I didn't think their father would be satisfied just hearing that we made a trip into town. He was probably going to want them to smile and volunteer that they had actually had fun. In other words, I was going to have to get them on board with the idea of fun as a useful and practical method of relaxation and rest. So I gritted my teeth and said as brightly as I was able, "Today we're going to have fun."

"Fun?" Rienne said.

Triste sighed. "Father again?"

Well. I hadn't expected that. They already knew the secret reason I'd been hired. Would that make things easier? Or much harder?

Rienne shook her head. "When will he learn?"

I didn't have an answer for that one. I also didn't have to give a speech anymore about the value of fun. Apparently they'd already heard it. So I opted to wield the nanny hammer. "We're going to town. End of story. It won't be that bad."

Through the magic of the computer intercom system I asked Havens if we could get a ride into Bar Harbor. The chauffeur was busy taking guests to the airport, but we arranged for Geoff to take us at noon, when he had to run in for some gardening supplies anyway. The gardening store was right next to an arcade, so I led the reluctant twins inside while Geoff did his shopping. I'd passed the arcade a zillion times with my dad and was never once tempted to go inside. But something told me Mr. Pertweath would approve. Maybe it was the word "fun" stenciled on the window. Three times.

Fun, apparently, requires a lot of coins and a lot of noise. The three of us stood watching the binging, trumpeting, chiming machines. I ignored the twins' horrified but mute pleas to escape before my insane idea deafened them forever. Fun. Yep. It said so on the sign.

Triste liked one game that involved shooting and fighting and required you to solve something to get to another level. Rienne liked the car simulator.

And what did I enjoy? That Geoff came to rescue me after an hour. He probably just considered that he was picking us up to take us home. I definitely considered it a rescue.

Of course, it wasn't the rescue I'd expected. He strolled into the place, breathed in deeply, and headed straight for the

Dance Dance Revolution machine. You know, the one where you play with your whole body, trying to follow loud music and flashing lights. I'd never thought much of making a fool of myself by trying to keep up with insanely paced music and flashing signals. Seemed pointless.

Until I watched Geoff handle the machine like a master—with a huge smile on his face. I couldn't help but smile too.

Apparently, Triste and Rienne were also impressed, because they stopped asking me if we could go and started watching Geoff dance. "How does he know how to . . . ?" Triste leaned forward. "Oh. I see."

Rienne also leaned forward, which was when I noticed I made three. I hoped Geoff didn't let it go to his head that all three of us were enthralled by him. But I suspected, from the looks he flashed me from time to time, that he was. Typical guy.

There was just something about him. Even when he started to glisten with sweat he didn't stop dancing. Maybe because Triste and Rienne clapped when he cleared the steps without any mistakes. Or maybe it was me that spurred him on.

Whatever, he danced till the end of the song and finished with a flourish and a bow. Then he held out his hand to us. "Who would like to join me for the next dance?"

All three of us shrank back. Geoff laughed and challenged me. "Come on. You want to show the girls some fun, don't you?"

No. No, I didn't. Really. I wanted Geoff to show the girls some fun and I wanted to take the credit for it.

I looked at Triste and Rienne and tried to pretend I would

have been willing to get up on that contraption. "Triste, you try it."

She shook her head. "You first. You're the nanny."

Darn. I *was* the nanny. Which meant one of my duties was to show them how to have fun. Too bad I'd forgotten how to let go and enjoy myself a long time ago. All I could think about was how stupid I was going to look trying to follow the arrows and the music and to jump, twist, and step.

Geoff wasn't going to let me wiggle out of it. He held out his hand to me, daring me with his eyes. I ignored his hand and got up on the platform next to him. "I've never done this before, so pick something slow," I said, wondering if Laurie was going to go nuclear over my dancing with her guy.

He grinned and slotted some coins. "As madam wishes."

"Slow" is a relative term. My score was nowhere near the "perfect" that he got. But I didn't fall off the platform, either. As a perk of being the nanny, I got to leap off when the song ended and send Rienne to try out her skills. Triste was next. By the time we left the place, we'd actually had a little fun. We were also hot, thirsty, and ready for a treat.

We went to Ben & Bill's for ice cream. More "fun." I had the macadamia brittle—and it was all the sweeter because I didn't have to listen to dad complain about the dentist bills looming in my future. And because Geoff was right there beside me, licking a chocolate chip cone and winking.

When we tossed our used napkins into the trash and headed for the door, I realized I didn't want to go. I wanted to stay there, in that moment, forever. I hoped Geoff felt that way too. Maybe it was my imagination, but I thought he looked a little sad when he said, "Time to go, girls," and we all climbed into the truck. Too bad he was into Laurie. Fun with Geoff was actually . . . fun.

When we came through the door at Chrysalis Cliff, I noticed the time. Oops. The girls were almost late for their family dinner. Still, we'd come in giggling, so I hoped our having had fun—even though it had come from me making a fool of myself—would give me points.

Laurie didn't seem to agree. She gaped at us for a moment, which was when I noticed the twins hadn't managed to clean all the ice cream from their faces. Oops, bad nanny. I'd have to remember to get some of those wet wipes to carry around with me.

"Sorry we're late. We went to the arcade to have some fun, stopped for ice cream, and lost track of time." Laurie gave me a dirty look and quickly grabbed the girls. All giggling stopped. Triste and Rienne put on their normal lugubrious faces and hurried into the family dining room.

I started to head upstairs, planning to ditch dinner for a shower, but Laurie came running after me. "Mr. Pertweath requires your presence at dinner. It's your job."

"Okay." Not really. I just wanted to go take a quick shower, change my sweaty clothes, and think about Geoff, the newly revealed dancing fool. I'd even considered using the time the twins were with their dad for a quick dip in the pool in the hope Geoff might be swooping leaves out of it. It would give me a chance to thank him for helping me find a way to get "fun" on the daily schedule.

I went into the dining room, expecting the kind of

dinnertime my dad and I had shared pre-Krystal. Some food, some pointed questions about school and homework, dessert. It wasn't always as grim as it sounds, though. Dad had even been known to whip up fancy ice cream sundaes for us, when he was nostalgic for his boyhood job at Dairy Queen.

The restaurantlike room was heavy and dimly lit, with the scents of dinner in the air. There was fluty music playing very low, almost impossible to hear. The dining room table was huge enough to seat twenty people. Mr. P sat at one end, Lady Buena Verde at the other. The twins were in the middle, looking lost in a sea of mahogany. Apparently I was going to throw off the symmetry, because my place was set beside Triste.

Lady Buena Verde was humming, but as soon as I sat down, the hum changed to a chant. "Free our spirits of sadness, O Great Mother. Free our spirits of sadness." She went on like that for a few minutes, which gave me time to realize that she was offering thanks for the meal. It also gave me time to wonder why Mr. Pertweath's domineering business partner was attending "family dinner." Poor Triste and Rienne clearly never got him to themselves.

Lady Buena Verde stopped chanting without warning, and my ears rang. Weird effect. Everyone else at the table had their eyes closed, but I kept mine slitted open because I didn't like the feeling of not being able to see. I didn't know these people at all, after all.

"Let us raise our hands up to the mother and release our gratitude to the sky." I followed the others and raised my hands but stopped short of wiggling my fingers like they were doing.

The food was served immediately: some kind of roast meat that smelled wonderfully of rosemary, potatoes that were small and crispy, and baby carrots and green beans. A balanced meal. I looked at the twins, wondering if they would eat it. Most of the kids I babysat for ate things like chicken nuggets, peanut butter sandwiches, and macaroni and cheese from a box. The girls ate without complaint. Dessert was blueberry gelato. Yum. And then . . . dinner was over. Mr. Pertweath hadn't asked the girls a single question about their day. He didn't even ask what we'd done to have our prescribed fun. He spent the whole dinner tapping at his laptop and nodding at Lady BV's business talk.

"The girls and I had fun today," I announced.

Mr. Pertweath smiled broadly. "How nice."

But instead of asking how we'd had fun, he turned back to his laptop, which ramped up my annoyed to full-on mad. I continued on as if he'd asked for details, as if he were a father who cared. "We went to an arcade and played Dance Dance Revolution. And we ate ice cream. Triste had the green tea flavor and Rienne tried celery."

Unbelievably, even the weirdo flavors of ice cream didn't catch his interest. "Wonderful," he said absently.

Yeah. Wonderful. Too bad he didn't notice how disappointed his daughters looked when he didn't even ask them if my report was true.

I thought about saying we'd also caught a killer whale, just to see if he was listening. I'd done that with my dad before. But my dad couldn't fire me. Mr. Pertweath didn't have to put up with me. So I didn't say anything.

Laurie hurried into the room and shepherded Mr. Pertweath and Lady BV to the next important thing on their schedules. I checked the grandfather clock. We hadn't been here even a half hour yet. Some family dinnertime.

I guess it was a good thing they'd asked me to join them for dinner, I thought, as the girls and I headed back up to our domain/ prison/witch's tower, since I'd have just about been in my bathing suit when it would have been time to retrieve the girls and get back into nanny mode. Not that I'd want to abandon them to the silence of that dining room alone. And next time, even if Lady Buena Verde glared, we were going to have a real conversation.

We passed by the pool, sparkling with light, and I sighed. Sometimes fathers are clueless.

CHAPTER EIGHT

A plunge into the brisk chill of the unknown can make even the most stalwart of nannies shiver and shake.
—Miss Adelaide Putnam to Daisy, the chambermaid,
Manor of Dark Dreams, p. 22

A few days later I was flipping through the Chrysalis Cliff brochure for the ten-thousandth time, trying not to go stir-crazy as the girls finished the Camp CSI work online. We hadn't left the building, or even strayed from our domain for a family dinner, since our excursion to the arcade. Since the girls' dad had shown so little interest in hearing about their mandatory fun, it seemed almost pointless to force them into more of it. But if I didn't find a way to get them away from their computers, I was in serious danger of spontaneous combustion.

There was a picture of the pool in the brochure, which made me desperate to go swimming. I loved pools, and I was determined to escape our domain, even if I had to twist the girls' arms and bend the rules to do it. The one loophole I could see was that the rules actually offered us a window of poolside opportunity, despite the fact that there was no time actually scheduled for us to use it.

Not that we'd been following the schedule to the letter so far. And swimming fit into the category of "fun" things to do. The girls had enjoyed our time at the arcade, so . . . "Who wants to go for a swim?"

They both looked around curiously as if someone else might say yes. Neither of them leaped up to go swim. I would have loved having a pool when I was their age.

I immediately realized that I should not have asked a question when I had no intention of entertaining "no" as an answer. But that was just a rookie error and could quickly be righted. Fortunately, I was the nanny. I opted not to debate but to dictate—one of the privileges of being the nanny that I was beginning to love. "Oh, well, let me rephrase that. We're going swimming."

I think mutiny might have been on their minds, but I wasn't about to succumb. I made them put on their bathing suits and get towels, and I braided their hair. But I also let them take books out with them because (a) I'm not a tyrant, and (b) I didn't want them to have revenge on their minds if I got flustered around Geoff, if he happened to be around while we were swimming.

The pool was a spalike grotto. A waterfall at one end created a sound barrier, and unlike the huge oblong pool I'd learned to swim in, this one was all curves, with a private nook behind the waterfall. I guessed it was the whole solitude thing again.

I tried to engage my reluctant charges, who were looking at the pool as if it were full of poison. "So much for laps. How do you swim in this thing?"

"We don't swim." Rienne was disdainful.

"You live with this beautiful pool and you don't swim?" I'd have been in the water until it froze over if I'd had a pool like this at their age.

Rienne went for the scathing observation. "It isn't very useful, swimming around in circles."

Triste nodded. "What's the point? You still have to shower, so you've gotten wet for nothing. We know *how* to swim, Pippa. But we choose not to."

Okay. I wasn't going to argue. It was looking less and less like I was going to be able to bill this activity as "fun" to anyone but me. And even for me it wasn't as fun as it could be since Geoff was nowhere around.

These two seemed to think everything out to an ultra-logical conclusion. I wondered if, in a few years, they'd be making their boyfriends crazy with their pragmatic decision-making process. Of course, puberty changes everything, as I knew firsthand. Wasn't I keeping an eye out for Geoff even when I knew he was Laurie's guy? Maybe the twins would be a little less logical and a lot more into the moment by the time they were interested in boys. Or maybe they'd save themselves the heartache and stay clear of the confusing boy-girl stuff.

The blue tiles of the pool shimmered with the movement of the water in the breeze, and I was drawn to the edge. I dove in without asking if the pool was heated. In Maine, doing that can be dangerous. Fortunately this pool was nicely warm. Even in the evening dusk I felt comfortable and soothed as I swam to the deep end and did a few underwater somersaults.

"I'm being pointless!" I called to Triste and Rienne. "Quick! Call the pointless police to arrest me."

They both looked up from their books for a moment, shook their identical heads, and went back to reading without comment.

"Don't you want to be pointless? Just once? It's fun." I paddled around lazily, thinking about what it must be like to be a paying guest.

All of a sudden Laurie appeared. "Philippa?"

I waved at her. "Hey, Laurie."

"What are you doing?"

"Swimming." I was tempted to say something snarky, but I didn't. Unless you count answering literally.

Her expression went sour. "Didn't you read the rules?"

"Yes." Call me petty, but I always enjoy setting rule-bound people straight when I'm in the right.

"The pool is for the patrons," she lectured.

I smiled and swirled my arms around, well aware that the girls were watching me, waiting to see if I would give in or fight. Duh. Once they knew me better they wouldn't wonder. "Actually, the pool is reserved for guests for most of the day, but the girls and I can use it from five a.m. to seven a.m."— as if—"and from seven p.m. to eight p.m., when the guests are celebrating their meal." Petty me, to quote the "rules" so precisely.

Of course, I'd underestimated Laurie. She smiled, and I knew I had missed something. "The girls are not swimming;

they are reading. Something they have no need to do by the pool."

"True. But they're in their bathing suits, so they may choose to swim." I could see Laurie was doing the same calculations I was doing. Evil nanny versus father's right-hand woman? I wasn't willing to bet I'd come out on top of that one. So I ducked under the water and took a second to think in the blank underwater moment.

I surfaced. "I'm going to teach the girls to swim. But it takes a little time, you know, to persuade them that it makes sense. They're really sensible creatures, if you haven't noticed."

Laurie grimaced at me. I think she meant it to be a smile, but it sooo was not. "Nevertheless, the rules are clear. You are the nanny. You cannot swim while the girls are left unattended."

"Have you ever heard the expression, 'You can lead a horse to water, but you can't make him drink'?" I made sure I sounded patient, though I had to try hard. The waterfall suddenly sounded much louder and less peaceful. The roaring of time, of injustice, of the forces of nature that didn't care a hill of beans about one sixteen-year-old and her desire to swim uninterrupted in the waters of life.

Behind me I heard a splash. I was tempted to turn around, but I didn't. I watched Laurie's face instead. She frowned in the direction of the splash. "Really. Those girls are not horses. I don't know what you think you're doing. I'll make sure Lady Buena Verde hears of this." She huffed off. Interesting, how she'd called on the authority of Lady Buena Verde even though she was employed by Mr. Pertweath. I couldn't help wondering if her loyalties were just a touch divided.

I turned. Triste was climbing out of the water. She was dripping wet and clearly not pleased about it, but still, she had gotten my back. I was glad one of them had. "Thanks for risking the wrath of the pointless police."

The dry twin, Rienne, shook her head and sighed at me. "Not at all pointless, Pippa. We don't like her any more than you do." Rienne put down her book and threw a towel at her soggy sister. "Only one of us needed to get in to make the point, though."

I certainly couldn't argue with that logic. How had they decided which of them would make the sacrifice? Coin toss? Short straw? Were they really reading each other's minds, like it sometimes seemed?

Recognizing that they'd had my back, I got theirs. I'd escaped the domain for a swim, and now it was time to make the twins happy and return. "I guess we can go back in now, before your lungs get too full of this fresh air."

"Horrors!" Triste smiled, though with only the barest up curve of her lips. Rienne met her smile with an identical one. I remembered how, after Mom died, everyone was always telling me to smile. People liked you better when you smiled; you made friends when you smiled. I'd ignored them since I didn't want people to like me for being fake happy and I didn't need shallow friends. I couldn't help wondering what it would have been like to have a twin, though. Maybe I wouldn't have minded Dad finding Krystal and starting to smile again.

Triste and Rienne scrabbled up in haste, grabbing books

and towels and jamming their feet into their sandals like they were being timed to see who could get ready faster. And then, all of a sudden, they froze. "Look!" Triste whispered.

On the flower bushes planted at the base of the waterfall were two butterflies. "I guess they wanted a change of scenery too," I joked. But neither girl offered even the ghost of a smile this time. They were intently staring at the butterflies.

"That's the butterfly I photographed for Camp CSI. The American Lady." Rienne pointed to the yellow and green one.

"It probably just looks like the same one," I said. But then I saw the gray butterfly beside it and I wasn't so sure. For some reason it felt creepy.

"I wish I had the camera," Triste said. "That Mourning Cloak looks like a ghost."

Rienne stepped closer to the butterflies, carefully. "Do you think it could be a ghost?"

My instinct was to say there were no such things as ghosts. That would be the normal response. If these were normal ten-year-olds. But this was Chrysalis Cliff. This was not the kind of household where normal worked. "Why would a butterfly ghost haunt here?" I said instead.

Triste looked at me in surprise. "Didn't you read the brochure information about our ghost?"

"No." Missed that. How did I miss that? Maybe I was too focused on the pictures of the gardens and pool and mud baths to read the fine print.

"This used to be a sea captain's house. One day, when the captain didn't come home from a trip, his wife threw herself off a cliff. He came back the next week, married a young pretty girl from the town, and had five children. The first wife has haunted here ever since, ruing her mistake."

Triste added, "We think she's the one who led Mother off the cliff. She's not a happy ghost. But nobody has ever described her as a butterfly ghost before."

Rienne stepped closer to the butterflies. "Do you think the other one might be Mother?" The hopeful look in her eyes struck me like a punch. I hadn't seen that one coming.

For a moment I couldn't even breathe. Mothers reincarnated as butterflies? I said, carefully, "I doubt it. Didn't you guys find out in your research that butterflies don't live very long?"

"True." They still didn't move, and we ended up watching the butterflies for another five minutes, until they fluttered off.

"Let's go. We don't want Laurie to chew us out again." We trekked back inside, glad not to run into Laurie hovering to make sure we vacated the pool before the spa patrons saw us.

Once we were back in the safety of our domain I made my case. Facts only: "Your father wants you to have fun. Your father is going to start worrying if you don't have fun. I could get fired if I don't get you to have fun." There. Three indisputable facts. How could they argue with that? Ha!

"We do have fun," Triste argued.

I felt for them. They were having fun in their own way. I totally got that because I'd been that way too, right up until Krystal starting sticking her nose into my business. Problem was, I had a job to do. A job I very much wanted to keep since it came with a fabulous shower and a pool with a waterfall. "I'm not talking about your perceptions. I'm talking about your father's perceptions."

"But father understands how much we enjoy our studies and our research," Triste explained.

Okay, so they were smart, but they hadn't really learned to read people yet if they thought that. Their father loved them, but abstractly, as if they were objects he could admire but not actually connect with.

"Besides, we already had fun that day at the arcade," Rienne chimed in.

"I think your father wants you to do things that could be classed as fun and would be more than a one-day trip somewhere."

"You mean like get a pet?" Rienne said, wrinkling her nose. That hadn't been what I had in mind, but maybe a small lizard or a goldfish wouldn't be a bad idea.

Triste shook her head. "A pet serves no purpose," she said dismissively.

No purpose? That I could argue. "It gets your father off your case. Makes him stop worrying about you." I felt my own brilliance in that argument even before the twins reluctantly nodded.

"That is worth something," Triste agreed. "Father already worries about his business too much since Mother died."

Rienne pursed her lips in profound thought and finally sighed. "True. If a pet will make Father less worried, then that is definitely a worthwhile purpose."

"Excellent. Then we'll get a pet." I was careful not to

phrase it as a question. Just the facts, ma'am. We were getting a pet.

Triste asked the expected question much sooner than I'd hoped. "But what kind of pet should we get?"

She wasn't asking me, she was asking Rienne. They stared at each other, and I realized this discussion was going to take a long time.

"Good question. Unfortunately, it's bedtime. Let's think about it overnight and decide what to get in the morning." Maybe by then I could think of a really great argument for fish. Or pet rocks.

In the morning I had an e-mail from Laurie that made the matter of a pet become priority number one. Mr. Pertweath was asking for an update on our mission for fun. Laurie's e-mail was short, and I wondered if she was still mad that Triste had decided to crush her nannies-shouldn't-swim-alone argument by leaping into the pool with me.

Please inform Mr. Pertweath of all fun activities that are occurring this week. Feel free to send an e-mail or update me personally at the end of each day.

Umm. Right. Why would he need a memo when I could just tell him over dinner? Or, better yet, the girls could tell him. I'd thought my dad was a workaholic, but Mr. P made him look like a loafer. Then again, my dad didn't have Lady Buena Verde breathing down his neck and telling him how to run his ship. The pet thing needed to go on the front burner.

The twins had apparently been giving it a lot of thought. "Maybe we shouldn't get a traditional pet, like a cat or a dog," Rienne said. "It seems cruel to get one only to pretend we're having fun. That kind of pet should be with someone who would really have fun with it."

"Just because we pretend the pet is for fun doesn't mean there aren't genuinely good reasons to get one," I told them. I didn't even offer illogical reasons, I spoke straight to their centers of common sense and practicality. "Having a pet can help lower your blood pressure, help you fight illness, and make you live a lot longer."

Unhelpfully, Triste added, "Unless you fall off a cliff."

"True." Or got in a car accident. "But that we can't help."

Rienne was in the mood to challenge me. "Sure we can: We can make certain not to get too close to the cliff."

I wasn't about to let them sidetrack me. I could be logical too. It was something my father—and more recently, Krystal—found exasperating. "There are things we can control and things we can't. You don't eat a menu of gummi worms and M&M's, now, do you?"

"Of course not, that's not a healthy diet."

"Exactly." It was nice to have kids who actually got the importance of common sense. "So, even though we can get hit by a bus anytime we're not looking, we still do everything we can to live forever."

"Nobody lives forever."

"No." We all sounded so sad. I was picturing my mom. No doubt they were picturing theirs.

After a second when I tried to pretend that the words

hadn't just sucked away all my enjoyment, I said, "A pet solves a lot of problems for us. Why don't we try it? If it doesn't work, we'll find a good home for the pet where people will have fun with it."

"Okay." They agreed with identical little sighs that said they were humoring me. Worked for me.

"Great! How about a goldfish?" It was fine with me that Rienne had already vetoed cats and dogs. You can't trust a cat, and I was deathly afraid of dogs. Not to mention, they smelled, bit, and, worst of all, licked your face when you weren't looking. "There's not a lot of room up here, but a fish tank would fit in nicely."

Triste and Rienne looked at each other, brows wrinkled and lips pursed. "Maybe." The zero enthusiasm wasn't encouraging.

"What else would you want as a pet? A rabbit? A hamster?" Either of those would be fine with me and easy enough for the girls to take care of.

"Good question. We need to do some research." They hopped on to the computer and started searching with the words "pet" and "practical."

Triste threw out a suggestion as she typed. "We could ask Geoff. He likes outdoorsy things. He might have a good idea." The girls shared one of those twin looks, which made me think the suggestion was slightly more than casual. Had they caught on to my crush? Or did they have crushes of their own?

"Great." Any reason to talk to Geoff was a good idea. "But we'll also need to check with Laurie. We should ask her first to make sure there aren't any no-pet rules."

Rienne gave me a look that said I was a clueless idiot.

"Laurie would want us to get a stuffed animal because it's less disruptive. Geoff's advice will be more reliable. He's a gardener, and he doesn't mind that a live pet might make noise."

Why did I get the feeling that Triste and Rienne were more interested in getting me and Geoff together than they were in getting Geoff's opinion on a pet?

I suspected I was in deep trouble, but I really couldn't say exactly what kind of trouble, or how to head it off.

CHAPTER NINE

You have been kind but firm with my children, Miss Putnam, and I thank you for it. However, this scheme of yours seems unwise to me. Are you certain you wish to continue along this path to certain disaster?

—Lord Dashwood to Miss Adelaide Putnam,
Manor of Dark Dreams, p. 63

I decided to check with Laurie about arranging for a visit to town to find a pet. I assumed Geoff could give us a ride, but a pet would need to be paid for and I had no clue how to arrange that—or even what a pet might cost. I waited until the twins had left for their music lesson, and then I headed for Mr. Pertweath's office.

All the discouragement I'd gotten from Lady Buena Verde and Laurie about leaving the domain made me feel a bit jumpy. But I wasn't a ten-year-old kid. I was the nanny, staff. I should be able to handle a trip downstairs without worrying that I'd disrupt the peace. But I walked quietly, listening for voices, prepared to leap into a closet or crouch down behind a piece of furniture to avoid being seen by a patron.

Even though I had an absolute need to seek out Laurie, the high polish of the marble floors, the faint scent of incense, and the worry that I would be seen made me feel as if I were trespassing on sacred ground. I hurried toward the office, hoping to conduct my business and be out of the way before Lady Buena Verde was any the wiser.

I still couldn't quite understand Lady Buena Verde. Did she just not like children? Did she resent them being a part of their father's life? Or did she actually think the twins would scare away patrons? In this house, children didn't even get the option of being seen, never mind heard. It didn't strike me as healthy, but I thought I'd wait until the end of the summer to let Mr. Pertweath know exactly how I felt about it. I really liked my shower and my personal fridge. Besides, like Addie in my mom's book, I was hoping to do a little positive family building between father and daughters this summer. Couldn't do that if I was fired, now could I?

Laurie was alone—no Lady Buena Verde, no cute brother David—but her smile faded a little when she saw it was me coming to bother her busy self. She held up her hand imperiously. "Wait here. I have to run an important errand." And then she was gone, leaving me standing there like an idiot.

She was masterful at alienating me, bringing back echoes of Krystal as she made over our house, switching out perfectly good paint, furniture, and carpet until I felt as if I'd walked into her house instead of mine. She'd always asked, though, before she changed anything. As if my opinion would change what she would do. I felt the same way when I talked to Laurie.

Laurie didn't hurry back to her desk. I stood there, the faint sound of "ohm" in the distance making me feel more stressed rather than less.

Just before I couldn't take it anymore and was about to bolt, Mr. Pertweath came in. He didn't seem upset to see me, which felt weird, since I'd gotten so used to the way Laurie and Lady Buena Verde jumped a little every time they saw me. Mr. Pertweath just said, "Hello, Philippa. Can I help you find something?"

"I was waiting for Laurie."

"Ah. She's assisting Lady Buena Verde at the moment. May I be of help?"

"No. I just wanted to discuss arranging to get the twins a pet." Since he looked confused, I clarified. "For fun, you know?"

"Excellent!" He beamed. "Have they decided on a puppy or a kitten? I had a dog myself when I was a boy."

"Well, actually, neither."

"What, then?" His eyebrows went up.

"Undecided." I shrugged. "They've been doing research. Looking for something practical as well as fun." I hoped that didn't sound like we were fudging the point of fun.

He nodded thoughtfully. "Interesting. Was this your idea?"

"The girls and I came up with it together. They thought it might be a good way to incorporate fun into their daily routine. More practical than coming up with a new kind of fun every single day." I couldn't help thinking that he should be hearing this from the twins. That he should be telling them stories of when he had a dog. I'd heard my dad's stories about his dog, Blue, so many times that I felt like I'd met the darned thing.

"Practical." He smiled. "I shouldn't have even had to ask."

"They'd be happy to tell you more if you wanted to come up this afternoon." I suddenly wanted to take the little bit of connection between father and daughters that I could see there and make a bigger connection. I held my breath hoping he would say yes. Hoping he wouldn't dismiss the idea without any consideration at all.

He cocked his head to the left, thinking. "Well, I might have a little free time—"

Just then Laurie returned, Lady Buena Verde in tow, like twin waterfalls to douse the weak ember of Mr. Pertweath's memory of having children who needed him. Lady Buena Verde was first. "Time? Today? I'm quite sure you have none."

Mr. Pertweath protested, "I thought, from two-thirty to—"

Laurie chimed in, with a few taps on her Blackberry, "One of our guests wants a private audience at two-thirty. I've just finished confirming." She looked at him. "She will be very annoyed if I have to shift her time with you, because that will interfere with her mud wrap."

Mr. Pertweath nodded, and I knew the twins weren't going to get a chance to bond with their father at all.

"Maybe we can discuss it tonight, then, at dinner?" No one could say I didn't give it a good try.

Laurie tapped her Blackberry. "Sorry, that won't work, either." She didn't look one bit sorry. "We're going to have to cancel the family dinner tonight and tomorrow night for certain."

"Again?" I blurted. So maybe I wasn't able to keep all my disapproval out of my voice, but I didn't actually frown. I don't think.

Mr. Pertweath ducked his head, just like my dad did when he felt guilty but wasn't going to change his mind. "Maybe later this week, when we're not so swamped."

"But—" I don't know why I didn't just give it up then, but I liked the girls, and I felt like I had to look out for them. Like maybe I was the only one looking out for them in this place.

Lady Buena Verde frowned at me. "Philippa, please. I only have a few minutes to brief Mr. Pertweath. Your job is to make things easier, not harder, is it not?"

Mr. Pertweath, surprisingly, defended me. "Philippa's done that very well so far." He smiled at me. "In fact, you've done so well in such a short time that I can say unequivocally that I trust your judgment. Arrange things with Laurie and let the twins have their pet. No sense waiting for me, they know what they need better than I do." He gave a weak smile and waved a hand as though to royally commend my soul to Laurie. He and Lady BV disappeared into his office without another word.

I'd always thought it would feel great to have an adult trust me. But it didn't. How could I possibly know his kids better than he did? I'd only been here a couple of weeks. Laurie must have been thinking the same thing, because she just stared at me, with both eyebrows raised. I had the feeling she was trying to decide what to do with me now that Mr. P had given me carte blanche on the pet situation.

"What did you need?" Laurie moved behind her desk and sat down at her computer as she spoke to me. I guess so I'd know her time was more valuable than a nanny's.

"The twins need to get into town to pick out a pet. I was wondering if I could have some money to pay for one."

She looked me over. "A pet?" She glanced at Mr. Pertweath's closed door. "He approved this without speaking to Lady Buena Verde, I gather." She sighed. "How much do you need?"

"How much do you think a pet would cost?"

Laurie shot me a "how should I know?" look.

"I haven't had a pet since my cat died, and my mother bought it, so I don't even know what it cost," I babbled. I'd gotten it on my sixth birthday. I'd wanted a kitten so badly. If I'd known they turned into troublesome cats, I wouldn't have begged so hard.

Laurie sighed. "Geoff has a company card so he can take care of the purchase. He'll need to drive you anyway, since the pet should not be transported in the Chrysalis Cliff limo. We can't risk it soiling the seats. You'll need to go in the truck." She punched up the twins' schedule on her computer, and cross-checked it with Geoff's schedule. "Good. The twins have fun time scheduled during Geoff's unassigned miscellaneous task time between two and four. Does that work for you?"

Like she cared. "Sure."

Suddenly I was sick of the tension between us. I decided it was up to me to pop the uptight bubble. "Thanks for setting this up. Hey, do you want to join us? Maybe we'll have time to hit the arcade again after." I wondered if Geoff had told her about the Dance Dance Revolution excursion. Maybe that was why she couldn't stand the sight of me—she knew I'd become friends with her guy.

Laurie did a 180 in attitude at the invitation. She actually smiled. "Sounds like fun." But then she shuffled some folders on her desk and muttered, "No time for play today, I'm afraid."

I shrugged, trying not to look happy that she wouldn't be able to join us. I think I'd be sick if I had to watch her and Geoff acting like boyfriend and girlfriend.

"Do they want a puppy or a kitten?" she asked. So now we were playing nice.

"Probably a kitten." I told the lie for one reason and one reason only: I liked knowing something she didn't. I didn't even feel guilty.

Laurie, clueless about my lie, just smiled. "I hope they get a Maine Coon. I had one when I was eight. Lady Alice Blue. She was the best cuddler, I miss her. You?"

I tried to get the disturbing picture of her cuddling with Geoff out of my mind. "Mine was good at causing trouble." Like escaping at inopportune times and causing mother-killing car accidents.

Laurie went back to her computer keyboard. "I'll let Geoff know. You can meet him in the garage. Be careful not to be seen."

"Great. We'll make sure to put on our invisibility cloaks. Don't want to scare the patrons."

Laurie smiled absently at my sarcasm, tapped her ear, and said, "Good morning. Chrysalis Cliff." After a pause, when I realized she hadn't lost her mind but answered a phone call, I turned away. "Of course, we'd be delighted. Personal attention and service are our hallmarks here at Chrysalis Cliff."

Right, I thought. Except when it came to two ten-year-old girls who needed attention from their dad.

CHAPTER TEN

A man of his responsibilities and station in life would never be interested in a governess, Miss Putnam. I hope you are not nursing tender feelings. I would so hate to see you hurt.
—Lady Deborah to Miss Adelaide Putnam,
Manor of Dark Dreams, p. 78

As we climbed into Geoff's truck a few hours later, Triste and Rienne asked his opinion on the best pet to get. Geoff suggested checking out what needed rescuing at the local animal shelter.

It was perfect—practical, sweet, kind. The Pertweaths could surely afford a purebred, but Geoff's suggestion made the pet idea much better. I remembered a trip my sixth-grade class had taken to a crowded animal shelter—for career day, of course. I had already crossed anything to do with animals off my list, so I wasn't remotely interested in being a vet, never mind a volunteer who cleaned out animal cages. Some of the kids liked it. Sarah had thought it was the coolest, most bubble-gum-pink thing we'd ever done on a school trip. Typical. But as soon as she heard she would need perfect grades to get into vet school, she totally tuned out.

"There are plenty of animals in need of rescue," Geoff pointed out.

"Yeah. We wouldn't need to call the pointless police if we knew we were adopting a pet and saving an innocent life." Triste, I was learning, was always ready to save the world.

"The pointless police?" Geoff asked, his eyes on the road.

"Pippa's phrase. It means the people who make silly rules and then think they need to be enforced because they've been made. Isn't it perfect?" Triste's approval made me feel a warm glow inside.

But not nearly as warm as the look Geoff sent me, and the admiring smile as he said, "Perfect."

"Pippa's smart for a nanny," Triste added happily.

I laughed. "Gee, thanks."

"We should at least look at the shelter." Rienne got us back on track. "Even if we don't find a pet there, we'll get ideas about what kind of pet we want."

There was one advantage to a shelter: It wouldn't have horses. I'd tried to persuade the twins that Lady Buena Verde would send back any animal that was bigger than she was or that would require a stable to be built, but I knew they still thought a horse would be good for transportation. I was advocating for something small and very easy to care for. Hamster sounded good. Gerbil maybe. After all, if Triste and Rienne got bored with taking care of the pet, as nanny, the pet responsibilities would fall to me. Triste and Rienne were pretty responsible as kids go, but they were kids, and used to having other people take care of less pleasant tasks like doing dishes and laundry. The maid came in every day, the cook sent our food up, all prepared and ready to eat. We sent the dirty dishes down for someone else to wash, and the dirty clothes, too.

The shelter was as quiet as a library when we first went in. To my surprise, Laurie's brother, David, stood behind the front desk. He recognized us right away. "Hey, escaped from the spa? Or did you take a wrong turn and need directions?"

I laughed. "Yes to the first, no to the second. We need a pet. I heard you have some here."

"Sure do, and I'd be happy to show you around."

I was surprised at how easily flirting came to me. Maybe it was because Geoff was standing there glowering at us. Like he wasn't dating the guy's sister. Awkward, much?

David led us into the back, where the quiet became punctuated with the sounds of animals of every kind. Mostly dogs and cats, of course. There was a really cute litter of kittens that looked like a cross between Siamese and Persian. Bright blue eyes and a tendency to climb into any available pocket.

"Whoa, there, no shoplifting," David said, plucking a kitten from my purse, where it had wormed its way under the flap.

The girls were not suckers for cuteness. They wandered past the cages lining both sides of the room, ticking off practical attributes and amount-of-care estimates like two little businesswomen.

David left us to go handle another customer, so Geoff and I stood side by side and watched the girls with tolerant amusement, something I knew all too well from the receiving end—people who wear a lot of black tend to get that kind of treatment from family and friends.

"Nanny gig working out for you?" Geoff petted the head of a puppy in a nearby cage.

"Those other nannies were just wimps."

He looked at me, a little longer than he needed to, and the sounds of the animals faded away to a faint buzz as the blood rushed to my head. "Yeah, they were. The girls are lucky to have you."

"I'm lucky to be here," I countered, hoping I didn't have a deer-in-headlights look going on, but afraid I did. "They're interesting kids."

"That they are," he agreed. "But you bring that out in them. They even talk to me now when I drive them to music lessons."

"They do?"

"Yep."

"What do they say?" I had a feeling I knew. They were trying to match me up with Geoff. The scary thing was trying to imagine what they would consider my good points. Had they told Geoff I was interested in black butterflies? Would that be a good thing, or way too weird for a guy who was into girls like Laurie?

"What you'd expect," he answered unhelpfully. "Practical stuff, except when they decide to read tarot cards or my palm."

Just then the girls came running over. "We've found her. The pet for us. She's perfect."

"Great!" I was glad for two reasons: One, I could get

a graceful exit from the uncomfortable conversation with Geoff, and two, the pet situation would be settled in time for my next report to Mr. P. But my happiness didn't last very long—just until I saw what was chewing on the wire of the cage the twins pointed to.

Who could have predicted that they'd fall in love with a goat? Not me, or I wouldn't have brought them within ten miles of the animal shelter. I'd rather have taken them down to the beach to adopt a clam. Geoff laughed out loud, but he seemed to be all for it.

Misty Gale was her name, according to the sign next to her cage. The twins, their practical little eyes glowing, were already warding off my objections with words like "useful," "purposeful," "eats grass," "goat cheese for breakfast."

I tried to protest. "It's too big. She can't live in our domain. And Lady Buena Verde will have a fit."

"I'll make a pen for it outside the garage. The patrons will never even see it." Geoff supported the twins, and I was outvoted three to one. I wished Laurie had been able to come with us. She'd have found a way to stop the madness. But Triste and Rienne already had their hearts set on the goat, and I couldn't be the bad guy on this one.

So we brought Misty Gale home with us. Fun.

Lady Buena Verde was not pleased, which we found out within ten minutes of Laurie catching sight of the truck pulling up, the goat standing tethered in the bed. I looked forward to a confrontation at the next family dinner. Mr. P wouldn't be able to focus on his laptop that night. And I doubted he'd be able to resist his daughters' happiness.

At least Misty Gale could eat grass and wouldn't require a stall mucker. If she did, I had every intention of making sure Geoff helped. After all, he had encouraged the twins to go for the goat. He'd seemed to think my horror was funny.

Once the twins were asleep that night, I decided to break a rule or two. I crept downstairs feeling a bit like a criminal, pausing to listen before turning corners and ready to retreat at any sound of voices or footsteps. But luck had returned to my life. I made it outside without even so much as a glimpse of Havens. The windows of Mr. Pertweath's office blazed with light—the man worked insane hours. I didn't think he would be able to see me, though, since outside it was completely dark.

There's something about a pool at night—especially a pool with a waterfall—that makes the darkness magical. Just in case Laurie or Lady Buena Verde had some kind of psychic alarm system to tell them when I wasn't where I was supposed to be, I lowered myself into the water with excruciating stealth, managing to avoid any splash that might alert someone that the pool was being used illicitly. The heated water cut the slight evening chill as I watched the ripples of my entry cross to the far side, glittering.

Enfolded, cuddling myself, I floated free, rocked gently by the waves I'd created. Heaven.

"Don't you know you shouldn't swim alone?"

Geoff. I tried to let the rocking peace hold me, keep me, but it was gone, replaced by the prickly chill of air on my stomach. Bikinis didn't cover much, not even in the shadows.

I let my feet sink and spread my arms to keep my head

above the water. Geoff stood in the shadows. I thought there might be a smirking tilt to his mouth but I couldn't be sure.

He lifted his shirt over his head with one swift movement and his body gleamed in the moonlight. Then he dove into the pool, sending a wave of water crashing against my equilibrium. I had to paddle harder and kick my feet to keep my head from going under.

When he came up, he was close, but not touching me. He shook the water from his hair. "You should have asked. I'd be your swim buddy."

Maybe that was what I wanted, but it definitely wasn't what I needed if I intended to stay out of trouble. I let myself sink under the surface, begging the complicated and frustrating world to fade away in the silence of the water. When I came up, I saw Geoff still there, treading water. I tried to picture Laurie, to slow the beat of my heart, but that only made it beat harder. The universe was perverse. I knew it, but never so clearly as in that moment. The thing I wanted most was floating inches from me and yet light-years away.

I felt exposed and vulnerable, and I didn't like it. "Thanks for helping out the girls today. I can't believe they picked a goat."

His soft laugh rippled over the water toward me.

I kept talking. Maybe it was babbling, even, because I felt safer whispering to him about the twins. "I've made them promise to do the goat chores at least once a day, so you don't get stuck doing everything."

"I don't mind."

I wasn't about to let that end the conversation. Then what

would we talk about? Or do? "Misty Gale is supposed to be their fun, so I think we need at least a daily dose, don't you?"

"Whatever you say; you're the nanny."

"I am, but just for the summer." I looked up at the stars. "You know, the girls really adore you." *Me too*, I added silently, but that wasn't going to come out of my mouth if I could help it. There was a splash but no answer. Geoff was gone. He wasn't under the water; he wasn't on the edge of the pool.

I'm not very good at letting mysteries go unsolved. Or, that was the excuse I used to search him out. I swam around, pausing often to listen and look. When the hand came out of the waterfall and waved at me, I nearly screamed.

Mad that he'd almost made me out myself for breaking the rules, I ducked under the waterfall and came into a quiet haven. Me. Geoff. Moonlight. It took me about one second to realize that while we were here no one could see us if they happened to walk by the pool, or even look out the window of Lady Buena Verde's office.

"Glad you decided to join me," he said.

"I thought you might be hurt." The excuse sounded even more ridiculous aloud than it had in my head.

There was enough ambient light coming through the waterfall to see him, but not well enough to make me nervous again. There was something about the way he looked at me that made me uncomfortable. It was nice to be semiblind in here.

"How noble. You came to rescue me." I could hear the sarcasm and was extra glad I couldn't see his expression.

"Or I just wanted a little under-the-radar time away from

Laurie's evil eye." I brought up her name on purpose. The intimacy was suffocating and the waterfall—or my heart—pounded so loudly I felt exposed.

Geoff moved closer, pushing water against me. "She's at my place, you're safe."

At his place? Could the situation be any clearer? "If she's at your place, why are you here?" I didn't want to ask why I was still here, I was too afraid of the answer to that one.

"She has this thing for that bachelor show." He dove under the water and did a somersault that pushed me away to the other side of the waterfall nook. He surfaced, splashing. "I can't stand that show."

What was there to say to that one? I opted for trite commentary. "So she loves you for your TV, then?"

He moved closer again. "Story of my life."

I pushed water so that it splashed against his chest. Maybe he'd get the message. "Yeah, well, I think Laurie's the one to talk to about that."

"Really?" He actually seemed surprised.

"Really. Go back and watch TV with her. Maybe the bachelor show will grow on you." Really. I wasn't a man stealer, even if I did hold my breath while I waited to hear what he would say next.

He didn't say anything. He dove under the waterfall and away from our little haven. I didn't follow. I wasn't a man stealer. Maybe if I said it often enough, it wouldn't seem like a bad thing.

I waited awhile to calm my heart before I, too, dove under the waterfall and came up in the pool again. The lights were still on in Mr. Pertweath's office, but no one stood at the window. Geoff was gone, as far as I could see, even though I came out of the pool feeling two little tingling spots on my back, as if someone was watching me. I tried to shake off the feeling, but it grew instead.

"Geoff, you creep!" I whispered, angry with him, angry with me, angry, I guess, with the world. There was a crackling sound from the bushes at the side of the pool. I searched for a sign of Geoff, seeing nothing until something white and wispy caught my eye. Geoff's towel? The fog moving in?

I followed, knowing it was a dumb thing to do, but knowing it didn't matter how dumb it was, I was doing it anyway. That darned stubbornness of mine kicking in, I guess.

I quickly realized that the sheer foolishness of my actions greatly exceeded my initial estimation of my dumbness. The lights around the pool disappeared a few steps into the brush, and the night was very dark, except for the light of the moon shining intermittently through the tops of the trees.

Nervously, I called out, "Geoff?"

No one answered, but I saw the flash of white again and let my growing stubbornness guide me forward.

I saw one more flash of white when the trees thinned out and hoped I'd get a glimpse of the house, Geoff, anything familiar. I had a tiny flashlight on my key ring, but I didn't think that little bit of light would be enough to get me home when I didn't know in what direction to point myself.

Stubbornness turned to panic as I quickened my pace and moved forward blindly. I might have wandered all night like that, twigs and brush grabbing at my towel, scratching my bare legs and arms, if I hadn't felt the ground slide out from under my feet. I launched myself backward, seeking firmer ground.

I'd wrapped the towel pretty tightly around my chest and stomach, but that didn't protect my legs from the sting as I slid, scraping over pebbles and dirt and low-growing plants. I counted it a victory when I grabbed onto a viny tree root and stopped my slide. After I'd scrambled back to level ground, I realized just how close I'd come to repeating history.

I'd come right up to the cliff where Mrs. Pertweath had fallen. I'd nearly reenacted the scene. What was the matter with me?

I sat there shaking for a moment as the fog rolled in for good this time. No sign of Geoff, and any ghosts would be invisible in the fog. At least I knew how to get back to the house—I could see the lights of the dock even through the thickening fog. I—carefully—followed a path that ran along the edge of the cliff to the dock, and pretty easily from there, I found the wide paved path that led back to the house.

Fortunately, no one was around when I slipped back into the house. I would not want to share my humiliation. Bad enough I'd gone out in the darkness, but to nearly fall off a cliff wasn't going to make anyone think I deserved an award for nanny of the year. Better to keep this quiet and resolve never to be so stupid again.

CHAPTER ELEVEN

Suddenly I found myself the sinecure of every eye. Not the place a drab governess wishes to be when she's wearing her second-best gown.
—Miss Adelaide Putnam, *Manor of Dark Dreams*, p. 102

For the next week I managed to follow the schedule almost perfectly. The twins researched the matter thoroughly, and we started the goat care I'd promised Geoff. He was a little cool to me but very helpful to the twins. The silence between us was good progress, I told myself. After all, no way could one guy be interested in both a girl like Laurie and a girl like me. It just wasn't possible.

At our next scheduled dinner, Lady Buena Verde chastised us as expected for choosing a pet so unsuitable for the spa.

Fortunately, we had figured out our defense and were ready when the salad course was cleared and the chicken was served and Mr. P—after a glance from Lady Buena Verde—cleared his throat and said, "I hear you decided on a goat as a pet?"

He looked at me, but the twins and I had already decided that Triste should answer and Rienne should do the follow-up. I'd told them I thought they could best explain their reasoning themselves, which appealed to their sense of practicality. No point telling them I really just thought it was time their father looked at his daughters and listened to what they said for at least a few minutes.

"A goat is the most practical pet," Triste began. "It eats grass, so there's less mowing. It gives milk, so we could have our own personal brand of goat cheese at the spa."

"Goat cheese?" Mr. P looked bemused, and I worried. But then he looked pleased, and I realized he had already been won over, without even much of a fight.

Lady Buena Verde must have sensed the same thing, because she cleared her throat daintily.

Mr. Pertweath glanced at her, but Rienne followed up on Triste's advantage. "We will keep her outside, near the garage, so she won't cause problems for the spa patrons. We have her in the rocky field that no one ever goes into."

Mr. P smiled at his daughters. "Just like your mother, practical to the nth degree. Chrysalis Cliff goat cheese, eh?"

They beamed. Triste offered shyly, "I've been looking at recipes, but I haven't picked one yet."

"No?" Mr. P started clacking on his laptop. I didn't have a second to be disappointed before both girls were up and standing at their father's side. All three stared avidly at the screen.

Triste pointed at something only the three of them could see on the screen. "Herbs are good. Geoff already grows a great garden for Cook. We could just plant a little more basil."

"I like the dried tomato recipe, too." Mr. Pertweath hugged his girls to him. "I'm proud of you both."

He looked at me, as a plate of fruit and cheese was passed around. "Thank you, Philippa. I knew I could trust you to oversee the pet decision."

"I just let the girls do what they do naturally," I said truthfully.

After a very pleasant—and almost hour-and-a-half-long—dinner, we left knowing that Misty Gale was safe from Lady Buena Verde.

As we rounded a corner, heading back to our domain, we came across Havens, speaking quietly to a patron. They both stopped talking to look at us, and the twins drew in their breath as one.

"Good evening," I said as I imagined Queen Elizabeth might, trying hard not to feel like a misbehaving puppy.

The patron smiled at us, especially the twins. "Hi." Obviously not all spa goers were child haters. I nodded back, coolly, feeling as if I'd nailed this nanny gig, at last. Unfortunately, my confidence got a good shake when we encountered Lady Buena Verde a few hours later. "One moment, Philippa," she called as the twins and I passed by an open doorway on our way back from an evening visit with Misty Gale. There was a storm brewing, a big one, and we were eager to get cozy inside with hot chocolate and books. I turned to see Lady BV standing by the fireplace, poised like an actress about to shoot a dramatic scene. More to the point, she was watching me. I wished Mr. P was around to run interference.

Was she still plotting how to get rid of Misty Gale? Had she discovered that I'd been in the pool at night when I shouldn't have been? I couldn't imagine that Geoff would have ratted me out. But maybe he'd said something to Laurie when he'd gotten back to his room and reclaimed his TV.

Lady BV cleared up the reason for her stare by saying, "Your aura is not so dark tonight, Philippa." Ever since Lady Buena Verde has said she sensed darkness in my aura, I'd been trying really hard to be invisible to her. Unfortunately, at the moment I was standing right in front of her. I decided the fastest way to get out of this conversation would be to just agree with whatever she said.

"We had a good day today," I said. "Our new goat, Misty Gale, has really helped bring some fun into our lives." Nobody who'd seen the twins handing Geoff printouts of how to care for a goat and increase its milk supply, not to mention how to turn said milk into cheese, would have believed me that our goat-care tasks were "fun" in the traditional sense of the word. Fortunately, the only ones in the room to see that were me and the twins. And we weren't talking. It was in our best interests to play innocent.

It was no secret that Lady Buena Verde was not happy that Mr. Pertweath had caved on the issue of Misty Gale, but she didn't say anything about that now. Instead she continued to stare at me with an intensity that almost had me convinced she really could see my aura. And that she didn't like what she saw.

Lady BV waved her hand. "A goat. We'll see how that goes. If it doesn't work out, Geoff will take care of it—only fair since it was his suggestion, right?" She smiled a brittle smile that gave the impression she was trying to be my friend. Creepy. She'd even somehow decided to blame Geoff for the goat instead of me. Almost accurate, but not the least comforting.

Out of the blue she leaned forward and demanded, "Have you seen the ghost?"

Shocked, I didn't answer right away. My mind blanked as I scrambled to decide what would be the right answer to such a question. Instinct told me the whole truth was a bad idea. Partial truth? But what part? And then the lights went out, a big slash of lightning lit the sky, and almost immediately, thunder rumbled overhead. The rain came down hard. I grabbed the twins' hands and wondered if we'd be out of luck getting up to our domain if the elevator wasn't working.

Laurie appeared with flashlights for each of us. Geoff was behind her, carrying a battery-operated lantern.

Lady Buena Verde said tersely, "Geoff, take the girls to their domain through the back staircase. I must go see to the patrons. Havens will get the backup generator up and running, and, Laurie, you contact the utility company to see how long before our electricity comes back online. Make sure they know how important it is." She swept out of the room, still spouting instruction, and Laurie followed.

Triste squeezed my hand and gasped. "What about Misty Gale? She must be so scared." If I hadn't held tight to her hand, she'd have been out the door.

Geoff bent down in front of the twins and said reassuringly, "Don't worry about her. I've put her in the storage shed for the storm, with lots of fresh-pulled grass."

"Excellent." I hadn't wanted to argue with a worried Triste. No way was I going out into the storm for a goat.

Geoff pulled open a door I'd never noticed and we followed him up a winding, narrow, and steep staircase that led to our domain.

The sound of thunder and rain—and hail, if I wasn't mistaken—outside was fierce. Wind, rain, high surf. Inside, we felt cocooned in the eye of the storm. With only the one lantern lighting our domain, it was shadowy and almost romantic. But if Geoff hadn't been there too, it probably would have felt straight-up creepy.

"Let's play chess," Triste said to Rienne.

"That's rude," Rienne argued. "Then what will Pippa and Geoff do?"

Geoff looked at me and smiled. I didn't smile back. He said, "Don't worry about us. We're fine." I don't know what else he would have said, because just then the door creaked open and Laurie came in. To my surprise, David was right behind her.

"Hey," he said softly, giving my arm a quick squeeze. I was grateful that the dim lighting masked my blush.

"I need to remember to tell Graciela to clean the staircase even though it isn't often used. I think I have cobwebs in my hair," Laurie said, pulling imaginary webs out of her hair as she spoke. "It looks like we might not get power back until morning. Are all of you okay up here?"

"Yup, doing great," Geoff reassured her—reassured all of us. "No ghosts or boogeymen in sight."

"Good." Laurie looked at me and then around the room,

as if she were just realizing that she'd stepped onto my turf for a change. I should have known that her entering my territory wouldn't change her bossy nature. I was, after all, just the nanny. "Mr. Pertweath suggested we all stay here for a little while, camp out together until the storm breaks. Got any games we can play by lantern light?"

In the end we gathered around the Ouija board. In hindsight it probably was a bad idea, but I didn't realize how bad an idea until our fingers were in place and Triste had asked the first question: "Are there ghosts here?"

The triangle glided across the board to "Maybe." Either the spirits, or David, had a droll sense of humor.

Rienne asked softly, into the darkness, "Mom? Are you my mother?"

The triangle didn't move. Thank heavens the joke wasn't being taken that far.

Triste sighed. "Are you related to someone here?"

This time the triangle moved steadily toward "Yes" and my stomach plummeted to my toes. "Stop." I was afraid. I didn't want to admit it, but from the looks that everyone gave me, they could hear it in my voice or see it in my face.

David lifted an eyebrow. "Easy, Philippa. We're just having fun."

"Let's have less spooky fun."

"But—"

"How about you give me a break?"

"Okay." David took his hands from the Ouija board. "Let's try telling ghost stories. You go first."

"Very funny." He was so not cute to me now.

Must Love Black   119

But I did go first. I told them what had happened to me the first night I arrived. The ghost at my window. The spooky command to "hellllp themmmm." Laurie looked unimpressed, but I could tell David and Geoff were wrapped up in the story, even though they didn't take it seriously. And Triste and Rienne sat spellbound and silent, staring at me with open mouths.

When I was done, Laurie took over and told a pretty lame story that I'd heard once before, about a ghost and a hitchhiker and a dark and stormy night. Then David told a funny one that even almost made Triste and Rienne smile, and I mostly forgave him for pushing the Ouija joke too far before. Soon it was Geoff's turn and I held my breath, waiting for him to start, when suddenly the overhead light flickered on.

"Power! Hooray!" Laurie jumped up in an instant and was pulling David out of our domain before my eyes even adjusted to the sudden brightness.

Geoff hung back, slowly gathering up the flashlights. "Hey, I know you're looking for something . . . useful . . . for the girls to do." He'd seen my warning look and had substituted a better word for "fun" since the girls were watching and listening.

"Always."

"I could take you guys sailing, if you'd like."

"That sounds like . . . it would be interesting." I tried to remember that he was only inviting me because of the twins. "But would it be safe?"

"I'm certified. I can even teach, if you want to learn."

"Where would you get a sailboat?" I started thinking about

the logistics to erase from my mind the images of Geoff and me in a sailboat under a brilliant blue sky. Sarah would so have busted me by now. She'd be packing the romantic picnic lunch and giving me tips about how to kiss a guy while wearing a hat and sunscreen.

He grinned. "This is Chrysalis Cliff."

"Oh. Right."

I looked at the twins. "What do you think, girls? Want to go sailing with Geoff?"

Triste said, "No, thank you." Rienne jabbed her with an elbow before I could say anything. The twins shared a calculating look and then Triste changed her tune. "Wait. On second thought, we do want to go sailing with you, Geoff. Don't you think he'll be a great instructor, Pippa? You could take private lessons if you like it."

I sighed and gave them the evil eye for their blatant matchmaking efforts, especially inappropriate since the suitor they'd chosen for me was already taken. But, sailing. With Geoff. I turned to him and tried to pretend I was agreeing for the girls' sakes. "You heard them. They're willing to put their lives in your hands, so I guess I am too."

"Great." He grinned and pressed the elevator button. "I'll have Laurie set it up and tell you when."

"Great." At the mention of Laurie, I had less enthusiasm. She hadn't really acted like a girlfriend at all during our ghost-story session. Maybe it was because the twins and her brother were around. Or maybe things weren't as definite as she had implied. Maybe it was time to ask? Too bad Geoff had already left.

The girls weren't going to let me think about Geoff. They wanted to interrogate me about ghosts. "Why didn't you tell us you saw a ghost the first night?" Rienne demanded.

Wishing I'd kept my big mouth shut, I answered with a shrug. "I thought I saw a ghost, but it was probably just the fog. Why should I have said anything?"

"It could be our mom's ghost."

Whoa. That wasn't something I had expected to hear. Although it made perfect sense once it was said out loud. They were only ten. And we all knew what it felt like to miss your mom so much you'd be happy to have her back, even as a patch of white fog that moaned at your window or floated into the woods and almost led you off a cliff. Which made me realize that I probably ought to disabuse them of the notion very quickly. "It wasn't your mom. It was probably that other ghost, the sea captain's wife."

"How do you know?"

I couldn't answer that one. They didn't know about my encounter with the second ghost, the one that almost got me killed. But I was pretty sure that nobody's mom would have done that. Luckily, they let the subject drop.

A week went by with no more mention of ghosts. And though we saw Geoff almost every day while seeing to our goat-tending duties, there was no more mention of a sailing trip, either. I kept hoping Geoff would bring it up, or that the sailing day would magically appear on the twins' schedule, but when neither happened I gave it up as a lost cause. Probably Geoff had forgotten he even offered, or else he mentioned it to Laurie and she reminded him that since he already had a girlfriend, he shouldn't be taking the nanny on a romantic excursion, even with two ten-year-olds in tow.

Triste and Rienne, though, had not forgotten, and they threw me a twist out of nowhere, in stereo, as usual. "We changed our minds about swimming."

"Changed your minds?" I asked. "I thought swimming was pointless."

"Triste found an article about a man whose boat foundered and he managed to swim to shore. We should practice our swimming before the sailing trip so we'll be strong enough to do that too."

"Oh. So you'd rather save yourselves than bob around in the sea waiting to be rescued when we go sailing with Geoff?" *If we go sailing with Geoff*, I added silently.

"Exactly!" Triste seemed pleased that I understood their thinking—as if I didn't know all about it.

"Wise decision, girls." They'd be proactive, plus I'd be able to bill it as "fun" to their dad. "I think we can work some swim time into our schedule."

Rienne handed me a copy of the schedule that had "morning reading" neatly crossed out and replaced by "swimming lessons."

Great. Nothing like starting immediately.

"Okay, we'll start tomorrow morning, but right now we're into your computer time."

They didn't like anything to interfere with computer time, so I wasn't surprised when they ran, excited, to the computers. But I was unprepared when they began to pull up instances of ghost sightings at Chrysalis Cliff.

"Do you think our mother could be a ghost too? Or do you think we're silly to think she's watching over us?" Triste asked quietly.

That question threw me for a loop. Talk about a loaded question. "I don't know if I believe in ghosts," I said. "It was fun to tell the ghost story when the lights went out, but I really think I just saw a patch of fog that night."

"I don't know if I believe either," Rienne concurred. "But we do regularly have guests who sight our ghost."

"So the brochure says," I said noncommittally. Mr. Pertweath was paying my salary, so I didn't want to be openly skeptical about something he'd printed in his brochure—or freak out his daughters by confirming it.

"I sometimes wish I could see it." Triste said sadly.

"Don't be silly," Rienne scolded.

"But if—"

"Only sad ghosts, with unfinished business, haunt the world—like the sea captain's first wife—if any do." Rienne was stern. They'd had this conversation before, many times, I could tell.

"But if—"

"Mom didn't have unfinished business."

"She fell off a cliff! She must have—"

"It's time for us to get ready for bed, isn't it?" Rienne cut her sister off and looked up at me.

I looked at my watch, happy to participate in the desperate attempt to stop the argument. Yep. "We'll have to table this discussion until tomorrow." Or never.

Sleep wasn't going to come for me, I realized, long after

I'd gotten the girls settled in. I opened the curtains at my window. Another summer storm had scrubbed the air fresh, and the gentle rain kept any fog at bay. I stood at my open window and dared any ghosts to show themselves. None did. I didn't know whether to be disappointed or relieved.

CHAPTER TWELVE

A woman must have confidence that she can trust others, or she will find herself lost in the misty uncertainty of isolation rather than solitude.
—Miss Adelaide Putnam, *Manor of Dark Dreams*, p. 128

Laurie was smiling when she saw me in the pool alone. Not so much when she saw the girls come blasting out from under the waterfall.

Or maybe I was wrong about what she thought, because she came to the edge of the pool and crouched down to offer the unexpected. "I've asked Mr. Pertweath if we can have some girl time and go shopping, just us two, this morning, while the twins are at their music lesson."

"Really?" So we were doing an about-face? I couldn't help wondering why. Had my possibly seeing a ghost made me friendworthy? Or did she want to tell me to my face that Geoff was never going to take me sailing and I should keep my paws off her man? I was going to have to hope for the friendworthy angle because I absolutely refused to get into a catfight over a guy. Period. End of story. No guy was worth that, not even Geoff.

I hesitated a bit longer than she liked, I guess, because she pointed to my black T-shirt and shorts slung across the back of a chair. "Let's go shopping. Get you out of those freak clothes."

I thought that was harsh coming from someone under twenty who actually wore neatly tailored business suits. Including pastels. "I don't—"

She interrupted, apparently uninterested in any answer but yes. "We can just be us girls."

I studied her expression. She seemed sincere. Girl time with Laurie? Why not? Maybe under the suit was a girl not that different from me. Or maybe I was just desperate after so many weeks without seeing Sarah, because I was surprisingly delighted by the idea. If I'd been a card-carrying goth, I'd have needed to burn my goth card in shame. But since I wasn't, all I needed to do was shrug and say, "Okay."

After all, I missed Sarah something awful, and the shopping in no way required me to buy anything that wasn't black. Maybe I'd even get the scoop on the relationship between Laurie and Geoff—if I could figure out how to ask without letting her know I was asking.

Laurie was trying hard to emulate Lady Buena Verde, and she took her job seriously. I guess I could tell she wanted to impress her boss, even if that meant doing things that might shove her into clothes and behavior that weren't her first choice. Maybe we could both use a little fun. I mentally smacked myself. I couldn't believe how much I'd been saying that word, "fun," lately. I hoped it wasn't catching. I liked the comfort of knowing the world was a dark place. Better not to get too happy and then have the worst happen when you aren't expecting it.

I also wanted to pick Laurie's brain about the ghost of the sea captain's wife. She had a lot more knowledge about the history of the house than I did. Geoff had told me that her family had lived in this town so long, her ancestors had attended the funeral of the sea captain's wife and his second wedding. I wasn't sure how useful hundred-year-old gossip would be, but I needed some facts to stop spooking myself out.

After I'd sent the girls off with Geoff, Laurie and I took the truck into Bar Harbor.

Laurie parked in a great two-hour spot, just enough time for us to do a little shopping and have lunch before the sleepy tourists came out to play and began to clog the sidewalks and streets. The people out at that time of day were mostly old folks and those with young kids. The kids my age were sleeping if they didn't have to work. Some of them, probably, even if they did.

Laurie and I maneuvered around the slow-going white-haired folk and the balky kids in need of morning naps, without breaking stride. I noticed she'd changed from the ambitious-assistant outfit into one more in keeping with her age—low-rise jeans and a low-cut tank top. So maybe that was the side of her that attracted Geoff?

It was nice to have money I'd earned myself and no one to spend it on but me, myself, and I. I felt a twinge of guilt that I wasn't going to get the twins a treat, but really, they had everything they wanted and more, at least when it came to stuff. If I could buy them some dad hours, I'd do it in bushels.

I looked around the town with fresh eyes—I could buy things. I could buy that painting of the whale if I wanted it. I didn't, but I could. I'd promised Dad that I'd put a huge chunk of my summer money away for college. Even putting money away left me with a nice walletful of cash for incidentals. Problem was, I didn't see anything I wanted. Until we came to a store I'd been in a million times with my mom and dad.

I didn't think for a second before I said, "I want to check out this place."

Laurie stopped. "A garden store?" She wrinkled her nose. Definitely not a fan of the garden, I guessed, no matter how much she was into the gardener.

"It was my mom's favorite." I'm not sure why I explained that to her. It wasn't her business that my mom had liked this store. Or that I still did. I was beginning to regret that I'd confessed my secret motivation to Laurie. It was a kitschy-cool store, with garden gnomes and coiled copper butterfly ornaments. And plants of course. But I'd come for the wind chimes. As soon as I had noticed the store, I knew what my room needed: a delicate wind chime hanging just outside my window to chase away the ghosts and the creepy-jeepies. To remind me that music was random and beautiful in the wind. To make the nanny room into Philippa's room.

I'd wanted one for a long time, but Dad had always

refused, saying they gave him a headache. Now that he'd married a woman who gave *me* a headache, I figured that meant I didn't have to consider his comfort when choosing a wind chime. And so I bought a smallish silver and gold wind chime that made a delicate tinkle that would wake me nicely every morning and gently lull me to sleep in ghost-free luxury.

Laurie came over, curious about my purchase. "Hmm. Goth girl is into wind chimes. I'd never have guessed."

"Yeah, well, I'd never have pictured you as the thong-out-of-the-pants type. What would Lady Buena Verde say?" I only meant to tease her a little. It's not like I thought it was any of my business if she wanted to walk down the street practically naked. But she seemed to get really angry and stalked away from me without a word.

I grabbed my change and my wind chime and followed her out. She had the keys to the truck, after all. "Hey! I'm just teasing. I'm not interested in being the fashion police."

Laurie relented and slowed down enough to let me catch up with her. "I know you think I'm just Lady Buena Verde's lapdog or something, but I'm not. This job is important to me, and I take it seriously. I don't need you judging me for that." Whoa. I knew I had to make nice.

"Sorry, Laurie. I don't mean to be making your life harder. I take my nanny duties seriously, too, you know?"

Laurie was less than appeased. "I'm not a kid anymore. You still have another year of high school left, but I'm done. This is my profession. I don't want to jeopardize it."

I realized I hadn't given a lot of thought to Laurie and her situation. She was a person, just like me, trying to survive. "You're not going to college?"

"I am, part-time. But this is the job I want. And I don't have a dad who'll send me to college. I have to pay my own way."

I'd never thought of myself as lucky before. But Dad was going to pay for my college, unless Krystal talked him out of it. As much as I disliked her, I didn't think she was that evil.

Laurie backtracked from her complaint a bit. "It's good for the character to make your own way, my mom says." She smiled. "I'd love to manage Chrysalis Cliff once I've earned my degree. It has so much potential. I know I could do a lot with it."

"Great." I didn't know what else to say.

"I have some innovative plans for the place," she said conspiratorially. "Geoff thinks they're brilliant."

"Really?" My stomach suddenly felt like a chunk of concrete.

Laurie nodded. "An outdoor yoga garden, like they have in spas out west. And a real stone massage, where the patron is on one of those people-size rocks on the beach. Doesn't that sound fabulous?"

"I guess." It wasn't anything I'd considered before. "But we don't have the weather they have in California."

"I know. We'd have to find a way to keep the rocks heated on cloudy days. But I bet we could do it."

"Have you asked Mr. Pertweath if he likes the idea? Or is it just something you talked about with Geoff?" I tried to ask the question in a way that would open the door for her to tell me just how close she and Geoff were.

Unfortunately, Laurie was focused on the great idea. "Lady Buena Verde says it might have some promise, but I haven't spoken to Mr. Pertweath yet."

"Lady Buena Verde should know. She's all about business, isn't she? They even do business at the dinner table."

"She's always like that, which is why she makes a good partner for Mr. Pertweath. He wouldn't work nearly as hard if he didn't have her keeping him on track."

"It doesn't hurt to stop and check out the butterflies now and then, you know?"

"So they say. I'm not so sure. Although I have wondered about how hard Lady Buena Verde works. For someone who's supposed to spread peace, she's not very good at leaving me in peace."

We laughed at that one. I couldn't help hoping Laurie might become an ally for Triste and Rienne. I'd be gone at the end of the summer, but Laurie would be staying at Chrysalis Cliff full-time. It wouldn't hurt to try to win her over to their side. "The girls could use a little more time with their dad than they're getting right now. And it kills me to see them so unfairly imprisoned in our domain. Something's got to give. They're little girls. They should be able to swim, to visit the butterfly garden—even to occasionally come down and ask their dad to help them solve a problem."

"Well," Laurie hedged. "I think Chrysalis Cliff takes a lot of attention to run."

"True." I thought of a win-win suggestion. "So, what if we

convince Mr. Pertweath to turn over some of his duties to you and schedule a little more time with his girls?"

That got her to smile a smile so wide and happy that I saw her left eyetooth was slightly crooked. Maybe that was what had charmed Geoff?

CHAPTER THIRTEEN

There are things in this world that even the most sensible among us fear to examine, Miss Putnam. I cannot yet say whether you are sensible or fearless.

—Lord Dashwood to Miss Adelaide Putnam,
Manor of Dark Dreams, p. 156

When the girls decide to tackle learning a subject, they're nothing if not relentless. When I got back from shopping, they were using the computers to research better swim techniques and how to perfect the most efficient strokes.

Triste explained their plans as she held the wind chime in place while I screwed it into my window frame. "We'll be sure to be very good swimmers by the end of the summer. Perhaps we may even join a team."

"Teamwork builds stamina," Rienne added. "You need stamina for all kinds of activities, including studying and problem solving, and of course swimming a mile or more."

"Yes, you do," I agreed.

I couldn't help noticing the difference in behavior they exhibited when they were enthusiastic about something. They were in their bathing suits and ready to go as soon as our scheduled swim time arrived each morning. I didn't have to cajole or remind—not even about sunscreen. They had rubbed it on each other before I could get the word "sunscreen" out of my mouth. Swimming might have counted as fun, but for Triste and Rienne it was very serious business.

Lady Buena Verde had noticed us, and several times I saw her standing under the shade of an awning over Mr. Pertweath's office window, watching us swim with an eagle eye. Every time I looked up, she smiled at me, but I didn't get a friendly vibe from her crossed arms.

There are some people who can seem as friendly as can be, but your fake radar—Sarah calls it fakedar—signal is so loud that you want to run away. Lady Buena Verde was sending my fakedar into hyperdrive. It didn't help that she looked like a giant towering over us as she approached the edge of the pool, peering down and smiling as if she thought it a grand idea that we were out in public where we could disrupt the peace of the patrons.

"Are the girls enjoying their swim?" she boomed down at me, still smiling.

I took pity on her nervous anxiety. "They're eager students when they get on board with the point of the lessons." I smiled back up at her, shading my eyes from the bright sun just over her shoulder. "We're almost finished with our session; we'll be out of here before the pool opens to guests."

She didn't indicate reassurance by relaxing her vigilant glance, but her smile got a touch wider as she recited the correct response. "Of course, I don't doubt it. You're doing a very fine job, Philippa."

"Thank you." So what if my fakedar was ringing alarms? With people like Lady Buena Verde, it's better to pretend they mean what they say. If you call them on their fakeness, they'll only try to convince you they're sincere and/or you're crazy. Lady Buena Verde and Krystal had quite a lot in common. Fortunately, my highly sensitive fakedar prepared me to deal with both of them.

"I don't say that lightly. I believe in saying positive things, but not meaningless ones." Okay, so Lady Buena Verde had fakedar of her own.

"Me too." I glanced at the twins, who were dividing their attention between perfectly executing swim strokes and watching me carefully, as if they were afraid I was about to be eaten by a shark. "Don't want to get ticketed by the pointless police for inane rambling, do we, girls?"

They grinned and came over to stand beside me, the sun sparkling on the water rills their movement created.

Lady Buena Verde shielded her eyes from the sunlight glinting off the water. Triste swirled the water even more. Smart girl.

I wondered if Lady BV knew that Laurie and I were in cahoots now. She was certainly smart enough to figure it out. Especially when Mr. P came out in casual clothes and said cheerfully, "Time to see to Misty Gale, girls." I had to admit, I hadn't thought Laurie would be able to convince him so quickly. Maybe he really did want to spend time with his girls, even though he didn't show it at all.

The three Pertweaths headed for the little pen that Geoff had built out by the garage for their goat without a backward glance at Lady Buena Verde. I climbed out of the pool, and Lady Buena Verde moved back a little, as if she was afraid her flowing silver silk would be ruined by the water. I knew from Geoff that the water was naturally purified by the movement of the waterfall, and so was not chlorinated, but I still had to put forth an effort to resist the urge to splash a little more than necessary.

I grabbed up my towel and my discarded clothes, probably faster than I might have if I wasn't in such a hurry to leave her sight. Strange how someone could beam at you and still make you feel you aren't welcome. It was an art, I guessed. I suppose if I watched her closely enough, I might learn to do it. I could definitely see how such a skill could be useful for senior year, when the cheerleaders started ragging on my fashion sense. Or, as they liked to call it, my fashion senselessness.

Just as I was about to follow the twins to the goat pen, Lady Buena Verde put her hand on my arm. Very lightly, like the quick slide of her silk wrap. "Philippa, I sense the shadow in your aura, as I've said before. There is a difference now, from when you first arrived. I must ask you again if there is anything I might do to help you?"

I shrugged and gave my standard answer. "I just like black. It doesn't mean anything."

"I'm not speaking of what you wear. I'm speaking of your aura. Your soul." She spoke condescendingly, as if only a child would need such a thing explained.

"I know what an aura is," I lied. I didn't feel guilty about the lie. As soon as I was safely back in my domain, I'd get the scoop from the Internet and the twins.

"Yours suggests you may have had a frightening encounter with the spirit world recently. I must ask: You haven't seen the ghost of the sea captain's wife, have you?"

I wasn't prepared for the question. I'd thought she was going to ask about my mom's death. That's what people who weren't into the woo-woo world did. Ask about grief and loss and sorrow. Not comfortable territory, but I'd been there plenty of times before, so I was prepared for it—a quick glance at the ground, a sad little sigh, and, "I'm going on as she would have wanted me to." That always handled the mom queries.

The ghost question? Not so much. So I did what I was infamous for at school. I told the truth. Plain, unvarnished, and probably not to my credit. "I may have seen it a few weeks ago."

"Where did you see it?" She leaned forward. Apparently she didn't share my doubts that I'd actually seen a ghost.

"By the woods near the pool." I hoped I wasn't going to get in trouble when she realized that meant I'd been disobeying the order to stay out of the public areas except during scheduled times.

"Really?" Her interest was well and truly piqued—the opposite of what I wanted.

I tried to minimize the damage. "Maybe. Or maybe I was just spooked out. You know, new place? Dark? Spookiness all around?"

"No." She shook her head. "I see it in your aura. You saw a

ghost. If you want me to help you take the shadows away, you need simply to ask."

Weird thing? She meant it. My fakedar was totally silent as she stood grasping my arm tightly and staring into my eyes.

"What can you do? It's just a ghost." Or not. "I'm sure it will find something better to do in a little while."

"I wouldn't count on that. It senses the sorrow in your soul, Philippa. You must act to rid yourself of the ghost's interest."

"Act how?" I pictured scenes from *The Exorcist* and shivered. I so was not going there. No way, no how.

"I can speak to it. Find out what it wants." She beamed. "Ask it to stop darkening your soul."

"Does that work?" I tried to picture it but failed completely.

"Oh, yes. It's as simple as arranging a séance."

She seemed too pleased with herself. I started to worry. Clearly, it would please Lady BV if I agreed to this séance. But frankly, a séance wasn't my idea of fun, fun, fun. Lady Buena Verde would just have to be disappointed. I thanked her, said no, politely but firmly, and walked off to join the Pertweaths and Geoff.

CHAPTER FOURTEEN

The storm came from nowhere. It swept away leaves and linens hanging in the sun to dry—and common sense.
—Miss Adelaide Putnam, *Manor of Dark Dreams*, p. 178

As I walked up to the goat pen, I noticed the busted fence. It wasn't the first time. Geoff had obviously recaptured Misty Gale, because she was tethered to a fence post. He was talking to the girls and Mr. P as I approached. They all stopped to look at me with chagrin. I wasn't sure how this had become my fault. The goat wasn't my idea of an ideal pet.

I rejected guilt by pointing to the guilty party, who was drinking from her water bucket as innocent as could be. "She escaped again?"

"Geoff says he thinks our goat is lonely," Triste said, a little triumphantly because Rienne and I had ignored her when she'd brought it up before.

Rienne still wasn't as tuned in to the goat vibes. "Lonely? That goat is just ornery. She doesn't want to do anything we want her to do. Has she given us any milk? No. How are we going to make cheese?"

"Give her a little time to get adjusted," Triste argued with her sister. "Wouldn't you be lonely if you didn't have me to keep you company?"

Rienne shrugged. "I guess. But I'm not a goat."

Triste said stubbornly, "We should get another goat so she has a friend. Then she wouldn't eat her fence and run away."

Another goat? I shuddered at the idea. "I think you're both right, girls."

"What do you mean?" they asked in unison, both staring at me with identically suspicious expressions. Apparently, they didn't like the suggestion that they both might be right.

"Triste, you're right that that Misty Gale is lonely." I turned to Rienne, cutting her off before she could argue why Triste was wrong. "And, Rienne, you're right that she still needs to adjust. Why don't we spend a little more time out here with her. She's doing okay now, with us standing near her."

Geoff, as always, made my job of minimizing the goat heartache difficult. I think he enjoyed it too. "She's not eating."

I stared at him, trying to send the mental message to get my back unless he wanted to be looking after another goat. "Sure she is. Look how short the grass is."

Triste wasn't prepared to ignore the problem of the escaping goat. "She ate okay the first couple weeks she was here, but she hasn't eaten for a few days now."

"How do you know that?" Mr. P was paying attention. Suddenly I could see the bright side of a lonesome goat.

Any other kid would have argued pointlessly. Not Triste. She pulled a ruler out of her pocket. "I've been measuring. I don't think she's eaten for at least three days."

Figures. I looked at Geoff, who was, not surprisingly, looking at me. The twins had that effect on people. I'd learned that it was no use trying to use platitudes with these girls. They liked the facts. I respected them for it, though I knew firsthand it was going to make their teenage years very rough.

Rienne conceded the not-eating point, her trust in her sister's measurement capabilities absolute. "Should we give her back? We don't want her to starve to death. That's not why we got a pet. And if she doesn't eat, she's never going to give us milk to make cheese."

I felt a little guilty offering a stall tactic, but I couldn't see any other choice. "Why don't we just hang out with her a little more and wait to see if she starts eating again?" It seemed like a good suggestion to me, except for the waiting part. I couldn't help sidling away from the goat a little. More father-daughter time, I told myself.

Neither of the twins were happy with that suggestion. Fortunately, Mr. Pertweath not only backed me up, he changed the subject quite effectively when he said, "I'll come out with you every morning after your swim time to keep an eye on her eating for a few more days."

Geoff broke in, "Don't forget, we don't know what she's been eating when she escapes."

Mr. P nodded. "Very true." And then, miracle of miracles, away from his laptop and the constant business pressures of Chrysalis Cliff, he sat in lotus position on the grass and pulled his daughters close. "Now, who's going to tell me about the sailing trip Laurie tells me you're planning to take?"

I turned toward Misty Gale so that Geoff wouldn't see me blush. Laurie had e-mailed me the schedule for the sail soon after our shopping trip, and I'd tried not to think of it every second of the day since. I'd been halfway successful. Sarah had managed to call me last night and had—long distance—helped me pick the perfect sailing-with-Geoff outfit. You'd be surprised at how an all-black wardrobe can offer a lot of choices.

The girls were thrilled at their dad's interest and launched into detailing the plan they'd already outlined three times—beginning with what they'd asked the cook to pack for our picnic.

Geoff whispered for my ear only, "You look nervous. Don't you trust I can get you out and back safely?"

I was nervous. I didn't know whether it was the sea or Geoff that unsettled me more. But I didn't want to let him know that, so I blinked twice and said very calmly, "Whether you can or not, the girls and I have decided we're going out only as far as we can swim back." That was part of the girls' plan, so I wasn't lying. However, they didn't have a clue what the real safety distance was, so it would be up to me. And I'd decide based on how Geoff sailed.

He raised an eyebrow at my comment, but didn't bother to reply. I guess his word limit for the day had been reached with all the talking about Misty Gale. Being a man of few words had to be a hard job, I realized.

After Mr. P stood up and brushed off his pants in indication that he had to get back to work—I was glad to notice that he actually seemed reluctant—we headed back to the house. It was computer time, I knew without having to look. I was really beginning to get the hang of this schedule thing.

The twins put aside all Camp CSI research and focused instead on goats, and lonely goats, for the rest of the afternoon. I never wanted to know another thing about a goat as long as I lived. But we did find a solution. Get another goat. Triste was pleased to the point of preening at her complete and utter vindication.

"Let's talk about it with Geoff tomorrow during our sail," Rienne said.

"And then we can talk to Father. I'm sure he'll agree. He's been so lonely since Mother died," Triste said thoughtfully. "He should understand."

All I could think was that Lady Buena Verde was not going to be happy.

On sailing day, Geoff met us downstairs after breakfast. "Ready to go?"

"All ready," I answered, though I didn't feel ready.

"Not quite," he countered.

"What? Do I have something in my teeth?"

"You need this." He handed me a life jacket.

"What's this?" I knew what it was, but I was stalling, trying to think of an excuse to get out of going. Suddenly, a day on a boat with Geoff seemed like a terrible idea. What if I got seasick?

Geoff grinned, apparently sensing my frantic desire to

back out. "Everyone on my boat needs a life jacket."

I looked around. "As far as I can see, I'm not on your boat."

Triste sighed at the inane argument that was keeping us from leaving. "Take it, Pippa. You're going to be. And if you keep arguing, we're going to be off schedule."

"Maybe I shouldn't come. Maybe I should keep Misty Gale company. She is lonely, after all."

"I told you she was afraid of sailing," Triste said to Geoff. Then she turned to me. "You said you hadn't ever sailed, and Geoff thought you might like to give it a try. You don't have to be afraid. We'll be with you."

"Please?" Rienne cut right through any logical arguments that were surfacing in my mind.

I sighed. "Okay." I supposed a bit of sun would be a good thing.

Sun might have been good, except we'd only just sailed out of the shelter of the bay and onto the ocean when the clouds swept in. I'd heard of a cloudburst before, but I'd never been directly under one—and in a sailboat.

Geoff and the twins struggled to get the sails down, and then he made sure everyone's life jackets were tightly secured before he yelled to me, "If we go over, grab the tarp and don't let go."

Go over? I didn't bother to ask it out loud, since the wind was whipping into my mouth every time I tried to breathe. I didn't even really want to know the answer to that one. I just wanted to hang on and not go over. But I did take a big wad of tarp in my hands, as did each of the twins, while we huddled so close together we were like one big wet wolf pack.

"Glad you practiced your swimming?" I asked Rienne. She smiled at me, bravely, I thought, for someone who wasn't dumb enough to believe her strokes were going to do her much good in this rough water.

As if the storm cloud wasn't bad enough, the waves seemed to be vying to see which one could reach the clouds first. I would have been sick, but I was much too scared.

Inevitably, a wave rolled us and we plunged into the sea. I kept hold of the tarp, even though it seemed a bit stupid since it was pulling me down. But Geoff had said . . . Just as I was grappling with the reality that I wouldn't be able to get my head above water and still keep the tarp from sinking to the bottom of the sea, I felt it lighten in my hand and I bobbed up for air. There were Geoff and Triste and Rienne, each holding a piece of the tarp. Geoff yelled something I couldn't hear, and started swimming toward—I had no idea toward what since I couldn't see. But I started swimming behind him and together we towed the twins behind us, with the tarp acting as a rope.

Eventually, we hit something hard and rough. Rock. I ignored the scrape of the rock face as I scrambled up behind Geoff. I turned and together we again used the tarp to pull the twins up with us.

We took shelter on the little rock that Geoff graciously called "the island." Our shelter from the wind and rain was the tarp we pulled over us and sat on, making sure not to leave a space for the wind to grip it and tear it—and us—off the granite face of our tiny island. With the tarp over our heads, the sounds of the storm and wind became muffled. We could talk without shouting; we could hear one another. We could touch one another. We pressed close under the tarp.

"So, anyone know any good scary stories?" Geoff joked.

"How about, there once was a sailboat full of people that turned over," I said.

"Keeled."

"Killed?"

"Keeled over. That's sailor talk."

"I'm no sailor."

"Sure you are. You just survived your first keel over, so you're official."

Geoff was determined to keep the girls' minds off the storm—and probably mine, too—so he launched into one funny story after another, about Misty Gale, about his family, about sailing adventures he'd been on as a kid. I probably wouldn't have said a word, except, when he delivered the punch line of his final tale, he pressed his hand against my knee. He pressed it and took it back quickly, but I felt the imprint burning there as if he hadn't.

Times like that call for babbling, at least, in my world they do. Maybe if Sarah had been around I might have put my hand on his knee. Or smacked him. Or shut up. But Sarah wasn't there. Geoff and the twins were, and I babbled. About poems, about wind chimes, about my mother, about black, white, and everything in between.

Under the tarp every breath and every movement that Geoff made seemed magnified. I found myself gratified when he laughed at my jokes, or shook his head, or squeezed my knee when I told about the car accident. Every time I started to think he might like me, though, really like me as a person, he would react in a way that confused me.

You'd think that being that close to a guy, a girl would figure out the score. But, no. By the time the sound of the wind stopped and the rain no longer beat against the tarp, I was more confused than ever about how Geoff felt about me. And about how exactly I wanted him to feel.

Fortunately, I didn't have a lot of time to fret about it. There was a more pressing matter—rescue from "the island." After the storm passed, we lifted the tarp and looked out on a sea that was calm and sparkling and beautiful. Our sailboat was nowhere to be seen, but Geoff didn't seem too concerned. He opened the case he'd hooked to his belt as soon as the storm hit us, took out a flare, lit it, and sent it up into the brilliant blue sky.

"Someone will come get us soon," he reassured the girls as he pulled out granola bars for them.

When he offered me one I shook my head. "I take it this isn't your first capsized sailboat?"

"What's life without a man-overboard moment every so often, ghost girl?"

I felt a chill. His smile was endearing, but the nickname? No, thank you. "I'd done fine without capsizing or ghostbusting before now. I'd be happy to return my life to normal status, believe me."

"Normal. Huh, I wouldn't think a girl like you would deign to speak that word." He grinned again.

I had felt so close to Geoff under that tarp. If I tried, I could still feel the press of his knee against mine. Did he like me? Or did he just think I was a funny, freaky ghost girl he could tease whenever he was bored or stranded on a rock in the middle of the ocean?

Apparently, our rocky island was a known hot spot for collecting those whose sailboats capsized in a storm. A lovely small yacht (not sail-powered) answered our flare and picked us up. As we headed home, Geoff said, "Keep an eye out for the lady, okay?" I didn't try that hard, and Triste spotted the floating hull and called out to Geoff.

To my surprise, he didn't hesitate; he just dove overboard, turned over the capsized sailboat, hoisted the sails, and headed in.

We weren't far behind him, and when we reached the bay I thanked the captain of the yacht who'd rescued us. Triste and Rienne also offered their thanks—solemn-eyed and sober, of course.

We climbed onto the dock, like regular yacht riders. No one could guess we'd been stranded, so there weren't a lot of nosy eyes on us. They were too busy admiring the yacht. Sure, we looked like we'd been put away wet and dried out in the sun, but so did most people who'd come in from the storm, so that was no biggie.

We sat for a while on the green, watching sailboats going in and out. Geoff brought us ice cream from the nearby Acadia Shops—green tea for the twins, mango for me, cherry chocolate chip for himself. At last, Triste said slyly, "That was fun, Pippa. We should do it again."

I laughed, hoping she was joking. With her, you just never could tell.

We felt like the four musketeers, having survived a terrible battle and celebrated our success with our favorite treat. We even toyed with idea of not telling anyone what had happened. We could always claim we'd taken in a movie, sheltered from the storm. No one needed to know. The truth would only make Mr. P worried and Lady Buena Verde annoyed. In the end, we decided we'd have to tell the truth. "Truth is less trouble than lies," Rienne said with such heartfelt logic we could only nod and wipe the ice cream drips off our legs.

It turned out that our "outing" had already been noted. While we'd been enjoying the yacht trip and the ice cream, Mr. P and Lady Buena Verde—via the panicked-but-trying-not-to-show-it Laurie—had been calling out the cavalry. Whoops. Our bad. Or at least, Lady BV seemed to think so. I'm not sure where she got the impression we intentionally got caught in a storm and almost drowned. Maybe the spirits were talking to her?

When we got home Mr. P came rushing up, Laurie behind him with her infernal Blackberry, and hugged the twins. Laurie went straight for Geoff, but I couldn't watch them because I had to answer a barrage of questions from Mr. Pertweath. The girls kept interrupting, but he wanted answers from me. The smiling, easygoing man was gone and in his place was a father who knew how close he'd come to losing his children.

Even if I lost my job, it was satisfying to see them, a knot of three, clinging tightly to one another, talking over one another. Like Mom and Dad and I had been before Mom died. The twins told him all about the adventure as he knelt on the ground for an unscheduled debriefing. I couldn't help noticing that the girls were very pleased to have their dad's full attention for a change.

"The storm came out of nowhere," Geoff tried to explain, but Laurie grabbed his hand and hauled him away.

She said, "Never mind. You're late to take our guests on the tour up to Katahdin, and they're not happy."

Sheesh. You'd think we'd been safe and warm, enjoying tea and crumpets, while they'd been stranded on a rock.

CHAPTER FIFTEEN

The man was most abominably maddening. One moment he seemed to hold her in the highest—and to be daringly truthful, warmest—regard. The next? He was flirting with the cook.
—Miss Adelaide Putnam, *Manor of Dark Dreams*, p. 22

Lady Buena Verde turned to me. I tried to slip away, but she grabbed my hands. "I sense you were protected out there."

"Yeah. Geoff did a great job."

"Not human protection; I sense a spirit-world intervention."

I debated whether to tell her that I'd heard my mother's voice in the wind, just as I was about to give up and let go of the tarp—maybe even stop swimming. But I couldn't. I shrugged. "You'd know that better than I do, I guess."

She stared at me, but I did the wide-eyed innocent thing and escaped upstairs to take a quick shower while the twins were still with their dad. I was sandy and salty and pretty frizzed out. I looked in the mirror and suddenly understood why Geoff hadn't declared his undying love. Man, I was a mess. I double washed my hair and applied conditioner twice, grateful for the six showerheads so I could fully desalt in sextuple time. By the time I got out of the shower and got dressed, I was presentable again. I was wearing black, after all.

I heard the twins calling for me, too polite to come into my room without an invitation. I came out of the bathroom and called to reassure them, "Here I am. Did you have fun with your dad?"

"Fun? No. But we did tell him all about the adventure." Triste wasn't going to give in to the word "fun." Not that I blamed her. Like I always say, fun is overrated.

I looked at their salted and frizzed hair and smiled. "Off to the showers with you. I think our schedule needs to bend for some serious cleanup."

Sarah called while the twins were in their showers. "Hey. Guess how many guys I've flirted with at one time on the site?"

"Twelve." I didn't wait for her to answer, knowing my news would trump hers. "Guess who got stranded on a rock with Geoff when our sailboat overturned?"

"Get out!" I had her full attention. "Spill."

I told her the important details, ending with the thing that had occupied my mind during the shower. "I wish I knew if he was serious about Laurie or not. He sends such mixed signals."

Sarah snorted. "Duh. Why don't you ask him?"

As the nanny, I had a free afternoon once every week. So far, I hadn't taken it. But Sarah had convinced me I needed to get away. I dropped the girls off at Mr. Pertweath's office. He'd really started stepping up and had even signed himself up for the newest session of Camp CSI with the girls. I announced to Laurie that I was taking my scheduled half day off per week, and bummed a ride from Geoff. He was heading into town to get more fencing for Misty Gale, who had escaped again that morning. I intended to drop a little of my paycheck on some cute new sandals and a second swimsuit because the girls and I were swimming every day.

Geoff was so sweet and so hot—and so frustrating—that I just couldn't stand what it felt like to be stuck in the truck with him without the twins to act as distractions and buffers. Sarah would have shrieked and rolled her eyes up into her head while silently screaming "Ask him." I couldn't ask if he was Laurie's guy. I just couldn't.

I remembered right before I reached out to turn on the radio that there was no radio. "Do you think we should bring Misty Gale back to the shelter?" I asked. Great subject. Let's talk about a lonely goat. But I didn't want to say what I really wanted to know—how much did he like Laurie? Was it just a casual, convenient type of relationship? Did I have a chance with him?

"I think she'll be okay, as long as she doesn't destroy something Lady Buena Verde values."

"What has she destroyed so far? Besides the fence, I mean?"

He looked sheepish. "Well, don't tell anyone, but she's munched on some of the plants by the pool, and she took out an entire bush in the butterfly garden."

"Wow. And you managed to keep that secret?"

"Of course. She doesn't mean to be a bad goat."

"How do you know that? Are you the goat whisperer?"

"Would that make you like me?"

Whoa. The conversation had veered off so unexpectedly that I couldn't speak. Crushes are so inconvenient sometimes. Being tongue-tied was a real bummer when you had nothing else to do but talk. So I pretended he was just a stone. A cute stone, but, hey. "I like you just fine. Who else would take me into town on a moment's notice so I can fritter away some of my nice big paycheck?"

He was quiet for a moment. But then he laughed and didn't try to return the conversation to the dangerous topic of how much I liked him. "I know what you mean. Mr. Pertweath pays well."

"I like the checks. And the shower. And the twins. But the rest . . ." I stopped. "It's a bit odd, living there."

He shrugged. "You get used to it."

"Good to know." Well, that conversation went nowhere. "So what are you going to do while I'm shopping?"

"I need to pick up some gardening tools. And some fencing for the goat."

"Thanks for taking care of her. I know she's been a pain, but she means a lot to Triste." I'd been wanting to thank him for a while. "Rienne probably wouldn't mind—" But just then, there was a popping sound and the car swerved and bumped. Geoff quickly pulled over. "Flat tire."

"Great. I hope you have Triple A."

He looked at me in surprise.

"What? My dad swears by them."

He grinned. "I can handle it."

I watched him change the flat, or at least try. It turned out the spare was uninflated too.

We spent a great hour waiting for the tow truck and avoiding the big conversational no-no: relationships.

"You have the perfect personality for a forest ranger," I joked. "You don't need to talk much, so you won't mind not seeing people for a few days at a time."

He grinned at me, but he didn't say anything.

I don't know if it was the sun, the stress, or the fumes from the cars blowing by us on the road, but I asked the question Sarah would have asked weeks ago. "So. Are you and Laurie serious?"

He blinked. Twice.

And then Laurie showed up right behind the tow truck and ruined it all by taking possession of Geoff and driving us to a small diner to treat us to lunch for our trauma.

We sat with burgers and fries and waited for the car place next door to put a brand-new set of tires on the car.

So much for spending quality time with Geoff. Or getting to town for some shopping. Sarah was never going to believe my failure when she managed to sneak a cell phone call and I filled her in.

CHAPTER SIXTEEN

Great success requires great risk. Have you what it takes to be great, my lord?
— Miss Adelaide Putnam to Lord Dashwood,
Manor of Dark Dreams, p. 222

Misty Gale was nowhere to be found. The twins and I looked for her until we had to go in for dinner.

Triste was quietly crying during the search. Every so often she would hiccup softly and say, "I knew she was lonely. I should have stayed out here with her. Now she thinks we hate her."

Rienne snorted. "She doesn't think we hate her. She's just looking for a friend."

"You don't know. You never even liked her."

"I would have liked her better if she gave us milk, but she wasn't a bad goat. Besides, everybody needs a friend, even a goat. We're lucky because we have each other, but other people have to make friends."

I don't know why her words made me want to cry. Maybe because I knew I'd have to face Geoff and know the answer. Funny thing, I'd finally found one time when I really didn't want to hurry to get where I was going and it involved a boy and whether he was dating someone. Go figure.

I tried to concentrate on the twins. "She wasn't a bad goat. But it's time for dinner; we have to go back. We can look for her tomorrow."

Triste protested. "But she'll be so scared out here all alone."

Rienne argued, "Look, she's a goat. She'll be okay for one night. She might even be safer out here than where Lady Buena Verde can get hold of her."

True enough. Although, looking at Triste's fresh wash of tears, I didn't think it comforted her at all.

The girls wanted to see their father. They needed him, and he probably needed them, whether he knew it or not. Before we could enter his office—Laurie, oddly, was not doing her usual guard duty—we heard voices.

"Do you understand the choice you are making?" Lady Buena Verde asked coldly.

"Fully." Mr. P sounded pretty cheerful for a man at the other end of Lady Buena Verde's displeasure. "And I only wish it didn't take a goat to make me realize what I should have known all along."

"So, the business isn't important to you, then?"

"Yes, it is." He sounded completely certain. "But my daughters are more important. Laurie has already taken over several of my jobs and she's doing fine work. I think it is time we promote her. Don't you?"

I heard Laurie gasp softly, just a tiny bit louder than the girls' startled intake of breath.

"Very well. Let it be on your head if the business fails."

Mr. P didn't answer because he was too busy hugging two very happy girls who'd burst into his office and run into his arms as soon as they'd understood what he was saying.

Mr. Pertweath told the girls that he'd help them find the goat and he'd get her a companion so she'd stop running away. They'd do it together. I confess I didn't listen too closely. I let it wash over me the same way I'd let wash over me all the things my dad and other people said to me in the weeks right after my mother's death.

I jerked back to awareness when Triste asked plaintively, "How do you know we'll find her?"

Mr. Pertweath didn't hesitate. "Because your mother is watching over us and she would never let anything bad happen to us. Or our goat. I know it." He picked up a picture of the four of them when they were a contented family. Only Mr. P was smiling, but I knew the twins well enough by now to know that they'd been fiercely content when that picture was taken. I suspected their mother—whose expression echoed theirs—had been as well.

All I could feel was a skeptical sadness. And then the two butterflies from the garden and the pool fluttered in through an open window and settled on top of the frame in Mr. Pertweath's hands.

We all stopped breathing for a long moment. And then the butterflies flew away, back to the garden. I wanted to follow.

The twins, however, hugged their father again. "Of course.

We'll find her," they said together. I don't know if they believed what their father had said about their mother, but the looks on their faces as they had stared at the butterflies in silent wonder made me suspect they believed with all their hearts. I didn't blame them. They needed to believe their mother was waiting, strong and fierce, watching over them with pride.

CHAPTER SEVENTEEN

The lost lamb is never lost to those who know it well, heart and soul.
—Miss Adelaide Putnam to Lord Dashwood,
Manor of Dark Dreams, p. 242

When we got back to our domain, the twins were already quietly plotting. I noticed they had printed out a topographical map of the area. I didn't ask. I just folded laundry, defragged the computer they weren't using, and quietly wondered if Geoff would always think of me as the worst nanny in the history of Chrysalis Cliff.

I guess they understood that I was unsure of their plan. Or maybe to them I was an outsider. I'd seen the three of them bond in a way I'd lost when my mom died. Or maybe when Dad married Krystal. It didn't matter when I'd lost it, just that I definitely had lost it. I didn't belong here; I didn't belong at home anymore. I was the outsider. On sufferance. Which really hurt for some reason, and made my throat so lumpy I couldn't swallow the excellent mac and cheese the cook had made.

I don't know if it was because I missed my own mother so much, because we'd talked about mothers more than usual lately, or because I was feeling lonely, but I did notice that my wind chime was noisier than usual—despite the fact that there was no wind. "I hope that's you, Mom." I climbed into bed. "Because I sure need someone to care about me in this loony bin."

My wind chime was noisy at the window. Usually that sound soothed me, made me think my mom was sending me good vibrations—literally. I asked her what I could do to help. The chimes kept tinkling. But the answer wasn't any clearer.

In the morning, things became very clear. Triste and Rienne were nowhere to be found. I didn't have to think for longer than ten seconds to know where they were. Looking for their lost pet, the ornery and troublesome Misty Gale.

Mr. Pertweath made me repeat myself three times before he finally understood the very stark fact: The twins were missing. At last, understanding, he said to Laurie, "Call the police at once."

Lady Buena Verde shook her head. She looked at me. "You, Philippa. You and your shadowed aura. You find the gardener, and the two of you bring those twins back to this house before noon." She said it as if she could not be disobeyed.

I didn't like being ordered around, but I wasn't inclined to argue with her, despite my horror at the thought of actually speaking to Geoff for the first time since asking the question that must not be spoken. "I'm on it." I glanced at Mr. Pertweath and added, "Don't worry. We'll find them. They're sensible girls. They were just worried about Misty Gale."

He didn't look as if he believed me, but I didn't blame him. I was relieved to hear him say, "You and Geoff take the property in the back; I'll take the car and check farther afield."

I headed off, trying not to be pessimistic. I hoped Geoff would be more optimistic. I really needed a dose of optimism right now, even if it came in very few words. Maybe just a hug. No, that was dangerous ground for the two of us right now.

Geoff didn't act different from usual when I found him in the goat pen, waiting for me. As I'd predicted, he didn't say much, just "Figures they'd pick a foggy day" and "I have my flashlight in case they're holed up in a cave or under some bushes."

It was breezy outside—a good sign that the fog would dissipate soon—and cold, so I shrugged on the jacket I'd grabbed before running down to report the twins were missing. The fog was so thick that I had an excuse to huddle close to Geoff, which wasn't a hug but was almost as comforting, without being pathetically needy. I tried to believe that my mother—and maybe the twins' mother—was hovering in the mist, guiding me to the twins.

We went all the way down to the dock, checking under every rock and bush big enough to hide a child or a goat—and some that weren't—but there was no sign of the twins. If we had been in a novel, we'd have found a lost scarf or a small footprint to keep us going. We found nothing, but we didn't stop. I was running on hope, maybe, or just the sound of the sea and the warm feel of Geoff's arm around me. Had I lost them?

We trudged back toward the house, hoping that they would have been found by the time we returned. Just before we went to admit defeat, the fog lifted and I saw a butterfly on a nearby rock. Not just any butterfly, the Mourning Cloak—the all-gray butterfly. I stopped dead. Geoff stopped too, looking to me for an explanation. I couldn't think of one that would possibly make sense, so I held my finger to my lips and waited.

I don't know how long we waited, but I know I was prepared to wait forever, with my eyes on that butterfly. Finally, we heard a goat bleat. Faint, but very clear.

We found them, all three of them, in a small cave, huddled together.

"You found Misty Gale." I said when they didn't immediately come out of the cave to greet us.

Geoff was smarter. "Why didn't you come home?"

"We're not going back if Lady Buena Verde intends to get rid of our goat." Triste was firm. Rienne tightened her arm around the goat's neck. I guess a night spent in a cave with a goat was a major bonding event.

I was reminded of the fact they were only ten by the stubborn way they stared at us. Where did they think they would live, go to school, eat, if they didn't go home? "Do you think your dad would let that happen? He's out looking for you and Misty Gale right now. He's already said he'd get a friend for her, too, remember?"

Triste was skeptical. "When Lady Buena Verde gets mad, even Father can't always stop her."

I finally understood my role as nanny, and knew I could master it this time. I plopped myself down by the girls and said, "The Mourning Cloak showed me where you were."

"It did?" Triste believed me first, then Rienne.

"I think you'll be okay if you go home. The Mourning Cloak wouldn't have ratted you out otherwise, don't you think?"

I couldn't tell if Geoff understood why the three of us were so sure a butterfly could keep us safe. But he understood about the goat problem and said, "I'll make sure Misty Gale never gets out of her pen again. Or the new friend you get her, either."

The girls scrambled out of their cave, dusting dirt and leaves off their black clothes. Misty Gale followed, blissfully unaware of all the trouble she'd caused.

Geoff was smiling at me. "You're pretty good at this. No wonder you haven't run screaming."

I smiled back but didn't say anything. I was good at this nanny thing and I wasn't going to pretend I didn't know it.

As we approached the house, we saw Mr. P at the pen and the girls ran toward him, pulling the reluctant goat between them. Geoff put his hand on my arm and stopped me a second. "Laurie and I are just friends."

To my surprise, I could look into his eyes with hardly any shame at all. "Good to hear it."

CHAPTER EIGHTEEN

Never forget that the end of one story is simply the start of another.
—Lord Dashwood to Miss Adelaide Putnam,
Manor of Dark Dreams, p. 321

My last day of nannyhood dawned blue and breezy. I had planned on following the schedule as usual, until I looked at the twins' disappointed faces and remembered something I think we all forgot much too easily: These girls were only ten years old. Their dad had been right—they needed fun, even if they didn't know it.

"It's time to blow this Popsicle stand," I said, heading for the elevator. "I don't care if you call it a domain or a prison, it's not where you need to be right now, is it?" I turned to see if they were following me. They were. And they were smiling. "Ready for fun, are you?"

"Ready to put myself right in the path of the pointless police." Triste said, and saluted me. Rienne curtsied.

We went by Laurie without a word. She was busy in her

new, much more responsible position. I don't know whether it was our grins or our noisy footsteps that made her break off the call and follow us.

Mr. Pertweath was hunched over his desk, staring at a set of legal documents. Definitely not fun. Lady Buena Verde was standing over him. And we came through the doors, three noisy kids who didn't plan on going away—or at least not going away quietly.

"We're going into Bar Harbor for ice cream, candy, and arcade games. Want to come?"

Lady Buena Verde said, "Out of the question. We have too much to do."

Laurie stepped in. "Mr. Pertweath, I think I can clear my schedule if you need me to take over business for the afternoon."

Geoff joined us, the keys dangling from his fingers. "I hear there are some challengers for my record at Dance Dance Revolution."

"Pippa will beat you this time." The twins were really spooky the way they chanted the challenge together and grinned their identical grins.

Geoff wrapped an arm around my shoulder. "Maybe she will, and maybe she won't."

"Maybe I will. Then what will you do?" I teased him.

"I guess I'll take you home, so I know where you live for when I stop by to see you every now and again."

I ignored the cell phone ringing in my pocket. It was only Sarah, and she'd just have to wait to hear the details until we were all done having fun.

Life is unfair. Mega unfair. And it's all my parents' fault. *I* certainly wouldn't choose to leave the house I was practically born in, not to mention all my friends, my school, my *world*. And just how sneaky was it to give me the cell phone I've been begging for since before I left for cheerleading camp (picture phone, text messaging, unlimited minutes, the works) just before dropping the bomb?

I should have known something was up. But, no. I was not prepared for them to spring the bad news—no, strike that. The *catastrophic* news.

We're moving. New state, new house, new school. No more sleepovers, no more a.m. gab fests with Maddie before school. No more . . . anything. Except, of course, magic. That I can have. As if I want it. My life has been just fine without magic for almost sixteen years. So why do I need it now?

Mom and Dad are lucky that they have me for their daughter. Ten years of academic excellence and five years of cheerleading have taught me how to handle any crisis like

Jane Bond—shaken, not stirred. Even when said crisis comes with a major twist.

I guess it's not surprising that, at almost four hundred years old, Mom thinks it's no big deal to uproot us. Witches think different, I learned that before I learned to walk. But Dad has no excuse. He's not even fifty yet, and he's mortal. He's attached to his things in a way witches outgrow around the hundredth birthday (or so says Mom when I ask why I can't have Dolce & Gabbana like the other kids).

I'd say my life is over, but I've used that line so often, it doesn't even get an eye roll from Dad. Would you believe Mom even did a little spell to make harp sounds play—just like she used to do back when I was thirteen and, I admit, a teensy-weensy bit of a whine-o-mat. And all I'd said, quite reasonably, was "I want to stay and live with Maddie until I graduate."

If only they were reasonable. But I guess I should know by now that *reasonable* is not one of the weapons in the parental arsenal.

Mom and Dad tried to softball the news that we were moving from Beverly Hills, California, to Salem, Massachusetts, by telling us our new house had an indoor pool. Big whoop. Our old house had an outdoor pool, no snow in the forecast for a zillion years, and Beverly Hills High School, where I was going to be the very first junior to be named head cheerleader and maybe, just maybe, run for student council.

"You'll be running your new high school before long," Mom teased, as if she thought swapping schools was as easy as swapping Swatch bands.

Dad was more serious, as always. "As long as you keep your grades up, we'll be happy, Prudence honey. We don't need you to be head cheerleader or elected to class government to know you're special."

Special. He says that word with a wince. Poor Dad. He never really got used to living with a witch or raising two children who could do magic. If I were a good daughter, unselfish and properly thinking of my family, I'd appreciate how hard it was for him to agree to my mother's request to take us to Salem, her birthplace, so that we could learn to use the magic that had been highly discouraged here in the mortal realm.

Why did they suddenly decide to make this move? Did Dad get a fabulous new job at his advertising company so Mom and I could splurge on shopping and spa weekends? As if. No. We're moving because of Dorklock—otherwise known as my younger brother, Tobias. When the hormones hit, he couldn't control his magic. After the third time poor Miss Samsky's skirt flew up in the middle of summer school math class, my mother had our house up for sale and my golden life at Beverly Hills High up in flames. Boys are dumb. Especially when they're twelve. I would have voted to send him away to magic boarding school. But I don't get a vote. Because life is unfair.

I think Dad was tempted. After all, he is a non-magical mortal who is much happier when there are strict rules against uncontrolled magic in the house. But the idea that my brother could go to a school where teachers would be able to do simple spells against his simpleton magic until he learns to control it was a strong argument. Besides, my mother said she'd move us to Salem with Dad or without him. And he really adores her, no matter how much magic makes him nervous.

Dorklock doesn't even mind that he's ruined our lives. He thinks it's cool that we'll be in Salem, living in the witch realm and able to use our magic without the usual restrictions we have in order to live with mortals. What can I say? He's a kid. He doesn't understand that, as the newbies in school, we'll be on a lower scale than even the lowliest freshman. Of course, he's used to being a scud, the lowest of the low.

But I'm not. I'm honor society. I was going to be head cheerleader. My life was supposed to be charmed, even with the big, bad magic prohibition. I had it all arranged—head cheerleader, and then maybe even class president. Fast-track ticket to the college of my choice in my pretty pink Coach bag. After all, I deserved it. I'd been working on being kewl since preschool. In Beverly Hills.

Thank goodness I know how to plan for the—majorly—unexpected. If I have to go (and apparently I do), I intend to keep my kewl. Even if I have to use magic to do it. Which is going to be a mondo change. Me, doing magic and not getting grounded for it.

But even I could not have prepared for just how fast our lives were about to change. The first thing that told me my life was going to do a midair flip in turbo speed was the actual day of departure. Instead of moving men and moving trucks, Mom flashed everything from our old house to our new house. One minute there, the next, gone. Dad kept watch at the window to make sure no nosy neighbors saw our insta-move.

Mom's sentimental and likes rituals, so we all stood in the living room and said farewell to the house. We sprinkled just a bit of incense to leave the next family a nice welcome, and then she said softly,

> "Bless this house and all its walls,
> We have lived here safe and sound.
> Now we move to our new home,
> Shift our things and cleanse this ground."

Zip zap. Empty rooms. Clean rooms. Fresh, blah cream paint on the walls. Even though the empty rooms of the house echoed and looked strange without all our furniture and knickknacks, I'd coped. But then I noticed that she hadn't just painted and cleaned with a zap.

"What happened to the lines on the door?" The careful nicks in the living room door frame that had charted my growth—and Dorklock's, of course—were gone. Missing. The wood was smooth, the paint perfect.

I'd been holding it together ever since Mom and Dad had said we were moving. No discussion. No appeals. No surprise. A cheerleader knows how to put a smile on, after all. But sometimes a girl's gotta let her true feelings be known so she doesn't get squashed flat like a frog on the freeway.

"The real estate agent will have an easier time selling the place if we leave it spiffed up," Dad said. "Wouldn't want someone new to have to do all the sanding and painting and such."

It was another sign that everything familiar was being turned upside down—Dad never calmly accepts Mom using "big" magic. Which is pretty much anything more than zapping an extra serving of popcorn if we run out and it's too late to run to the market. Normally I'd suspect him of taking a couple of Xanax, but he was about to drive and he doesn't even take an antihistamine if he's going to be behind the wheel. My dad makes a square look like it has sloppy corners.

"Put it back." I looked at Mom. "It's the house's character. You've said so a million times."

"It's only a thing, sweetheart. Remember, things are not important, people are. And the new people will make their own memories and create their own character for this house."

"It's not fair!" I whined. Harps sounded, mocking my words. *It's not fair.* I tried to shoot the thoughts through my blazing eyes. I think it worked, because my parents looked taken aback. And harp music didn't play.

"That's enough out of you, young lady," my dad said. The move had gotten on his nerves too. "Get out to the car right now."

I thought about making a grand gesture—running off to my room, slamming my door, refusing to go. But the room was empty. All my stuff was gone to the new house. Grand gestures shouldn't be wasted. We only get so many in one lifetime (or so says Grandmama, Queen of High Drama).

"Time to go." Mom was grimly cheerful. She was usually the optimist to his pessimist. But I think leaving was hard for her. This was her first home with my dad. Where she'd raised us. She was going back home, sort of. But I don't think she liked it. Not that she was going to do less than she thought was right for her children.

Too bad she didn't believe in witch boot camp. Dorklock was the perfect candidate. He was already out in the SUV, just waiting to go. He didn't even mind leaving everything behind. He'd like boot camp. It was the perfect solution. Apparently, in her eyes, perfect mothers didn't send their imperfect children away. Too bad she couldn't see the situation through my eyes.

Then again, maybe she did, a little. She put her arm around me and led me out. As we passed the door, she touched the spot where the notches had been and they reappeared. "Even a new family can enjoy a little lingering character."

"Just a minute." I stood there looking at the naked rooms that weren't anything like home anymore. I touched the top notch, and my name, PRUDENCE, appeared in the wood. Not to leave the Dorklock out, although he probably deserved it, I touched his top line and his name, TOBIAS, appeared. His top line was only a little under mine, despite the fact that he's four years younger. Soon he would be taller. Would there be a door frame to notch in the new house? And did it matter, when it wasn't home and never would be?

For a moment, I considered locking the front door to the house and refusing to leave. But, seriously, I'm in it to win it, just like a good cheerleader should be. What was there to win in refusing to go? An empty house that wasn't ours anymore? All my things were far away, in Salem.

Still, it was hard not to revert to the Terrible Twos. And I guess it showed, because when Dad came back he gave Mom that "Is she sane?" look they like to use when they think I'm being unreasonable. "Ready, princess?"

Princess? More like medieval serf. It's a wonder I'm a leader at school, considering how they treat me like a baby. I tried not to cry. Crying makes my voice shake. And voice-shaking is not leadership-quality behavior. I may have been forced to leave my cheerleading squad behind, but I would go with head high and a big fake smile in place. If only—

"We're going to come back," I began. "Why can't we just leave the house . . ."

"I'm not made of money, princess. We'll make a nice profit on the house. That's how we can afford the pool in the new place."

Pool. Big deal. Although, I suppose it could come in handy in establishing kewl status in Salem.

I walked out the door, fighting tears, to see a dozen girls in cheerleading uniforms on the lawn Tobias had just mowed for the last time this morning. The whole A squad. All sixteen of them, including Chezzie, who hates me, and Maddie, my best friend. In full gear.

All I could think for a second was that I needed to grab my uniform and fall in line. But I'd turned my uniform in to Coach. In the heartbeat it took for the gut-punch to hit me that I was no longer a part of the squad, that it was complete without me, they geared up and began a cheer.

"Gimme a B!"

"Gimme a Y!"

"Gimme an E!"

"Noooooooooooooooooooooo."

"We love Pru so so much."

"We can't let her goooooo."

"So come back soon and we'll cheer."

"For Pru, our leader dear."

I didn't want to cry, because Chezzie was watching and she'd tell everyone, including Brent, my crush du jour. I'd been planning to wage a campaign to get him to take me to the junior prom this year. It was bad enough that I had to leave without knowing if the definite buzz between Brent and me would turn into a nice hot relationship. I didn't need Chezzie talking to him and making sure he wouldn't talk to me if I *did* manage to talk Mom and Dad into coming back. I could just imagine, "She was so jealous of how good we looked without her, she was screaming with rage." Chezzie puts the yotch in beeyotch.

Not that Chezzie would be wrong. I *was* jealous of them. Jealous that their worlds weren't being ripped into confetti. Jealous that they weren't going to have to piece all the confetti together again in another place and put on a smile while doing it.

So by the time the cheer ended, I'd managed to stop the waterworks. My cheeks were wet and I know my mascara was probably running, but at least I wasn't squirting tears like an insane teenage water fountain. I wish I'd thought to put on waterproof mascara, but I hadn't been planning to swim—or cry my eyes out either.

The squad stood for a moment in ready position, like we'd all been taught: take the bow, accept the appreciation, be proud. I had about a nanosecond to respond, and the wrong response could mean I'd be lower than a scud if I was lucky enough to convince my parents to come back home where we belonged. Reputation is precious, and I didn't want to lose mine in the last sixty seconds I lived in Beverly Hills.

"You guys!" I ran to hug them before they could move toward me. "I'm going to miss you!" I really was going to miss everyone but Chezzie, the snake with fake double-D's, but there was no point saying so out loud. Truth is, a good head cheerleader knows her team, and I knew mine, good and bad.

Maddie ran to meet me and we hugged. There were tears in her eyes and her embrace was no weak-armed "let me see whether you have silicone or saline" hug. She grabbed me like she wasn't going to let me go. Now I had an excuse for my drippy mascara. She whispered, "Run away and I'll sneak you into my closet. No one will know."

"My mom knows everything." It's a standing joke with my friends and enemies alike that my mother knows what I do before I do it. They don't know the half of it. Mom has those CIA tracking devices in the movies beat—she's set so many protective spells over me, it's amazing I can walk or talk half the time.

"I'll distract her. You run. 'Cause I don't think I can face junior year without you." That's Maddie, trying to cheer me up by letting me know how miserable she is. "You'll be fine. Look at what a great cheer you just gave." Besides, she wasn't changing schools and didn't have to snarf up kewl status from squat. But there was no point sour-graping her. It wasn't her fault I was moving. And she *had* offered me her closet.

"But you've been working on the cheer routine all summer. All we did was tweak it to fit today."

Trust Maddie to think that would make me feel better. I'd given her the notebook with all my routines and the music. Not that Maddie would ever be captain of the squad. She's a mouse when it comes to leadership. She's a great right hand, and I wish I could pack her in my suitcase, but I only gave her the notebook because I couldn't bear to give it to Chezzie.

I hugged her tight. "I'm going to miss you most of all. Don't forget to text me everything that's happening."

"You too." She glanced at my dad, who was making shooing motions toward the car. "Maybe you can come back soon."

"Maybe." I didn't try to sound hopeful. I wasn't.

"The team thought you should have this." Chezzie walked up to us and thrust a package with a big bow on it at me. "Salem—isn't that where the witches were? That should make you feel at home."

Chezzie and I used to be best friends. Until I told her I was a witch and she pulled out her cross and holy water and started to exorcise me. Picture me and Chezzie, about eight. She has a pink plastic bottle of holy water and a matching lavender cross. I have a horrified expression.

Even though Mom wiped her memory, mine is still intact. Chezzie is prejudiced, and I'm just not up with that.

Not that she remembers I'm a real witch, of course. But something stuck, because if she's not calling me a bitch, she's calling me a witch. It'll be interesting to see what witches call one another when they're PMSing. Mortals? I don't think so.

Chezzie was smiling and acting like she was joking, but I knew better. I unwrapped the package to find a shiny new Splitflex. Perfect for the girl without a cheerleading squad. Still, I hugged her and laughed. "Good luck to all of you—and be good to your new captain, whoever she is."

That dimmed Chezzie's bleached-bright grin. But only for a second. "Oh, I'll make sure they are. And don't worry, I'll be a good captain, maybe even better than you would have been."

"Ouch," interjected Sarah, a strong girl who could hold and throw like a guy and had about as much sensitivity to girl-speak. "Is that your way of saying, 'Don't let the door hit you in the butt on your way out'?"

Maddie frowned at her. But after I had torn up my uniform and had to zap it back together to hand in to Coach, I had accepted that fate had spoken. I wasn't going to be the youngest head cheerleader of the Beverly Hills High School squad. It was a size-zero comfort that Chezzie was a senior, so she wouldn't be taking everything from me—just the work, the fun, and the glory. "Chezzie, I wish you all the votes you deserve, girl. And I look forward to seeing you in the finals."

She looked surprised. They all did. "You mean you'd be a cheerleader on another school's squad?"

Truth time? The thought hadn't even occurred to me until it came out to pop Chezzie's gloat balloon. Finals? Against BHHS? "Duh? Why not? If I have to go to Salem, why not teach them to act Beverly Hills? Besides"—I held up the Splitflex—"I have this to keep my splits in perfect form. It would be a shame to waste it."

From the looks on their faces, you'd think I'd said I was going to go on *Oprah* and tell all their secrets on national TV. As if anyone really wanted to know.

"Thanks for giving us such a great send-off, girls," my dad said, tapping his watch. "But we have a schedule to keep."

"Right." I climbed into the SUV and strapped in. I waved until I was out of sight, trying not to think about how I would face a new school without Maddie to help me pick out my clothes and pluck the stray eyebrows I sometimes forgot. And . . . never mind. It doesn't matter. I'm going to Salem. And maybe I would meet them at the tournament. But I wish I hadn't said so. Because my comment had changed something. I could see it in the way Chezzie's top front teeth had peeked out of her smile like they did when she thought she had juicy news to tell.

And I could feel it inside me. Would I be a traitor if I cheered against them? It wasn't my fault I had to go to a new school. And I intended to be kewl, no matter what it took—even if it did come down to beating Beverly Hills in the cheerleading finals.

"First stop, Grand Canyon!" Dad announced. Oh, goody. I put in my earphones and turned up the music, the oh-so-appropriate "Boulevard of Broken Dreams," by Green Day. Prepare for a bumpy ride, I thought. Life is so not fair.

ABOUT THE AUTHOR

Kelly McClymer's passion has been writing ever since her sixth-grade essay on how not to bake bread earned her an A-plus. After cleaning up the doughy mess, she gave up bread making for good and turned to writing and teaching as creative outlets. Kelly is the author of numerous adult romances, as well as *The Salem Witch Tryouts, Competition's a Witch, She's a Witch Girl*, and *Getting to Third Date*. She lives in Maine with her husband and three children. Visit her online at kellymcclymer.com.

Public Displays
of
Confession

Lauren Barnholdt   Randi Reisfeld   Leslie Margolis

Like a guilty-pleasure celeb magazine,
these juicy Hollywood stories
will suck you right in. . . .

★ ★ ★

FROM SIMON PULSE ♥ PUBLISHED BY SIMON & SCHUSTER